ERRI DE LUCA is an Italian write[r]  awards include the Prix Femina, t[he Euro]pean Book Prize and the Europea[n ... His books] have been translated into more th[an ... A keen] mountain climber, he lives in the c[ountry]side near Rome.

N. S. THOMPSON is a poet, writer and translator. He lives near Oxford.

"The only true first-rate writer that the new millennium has given to Italy" *Corriere della Sera*

"A plot summary does not do justice to the way in which this almost skeletal narrative captivates. The writing is equally spare, but has a profound lyric intensity ... transfixing" *Spectator Australia*

"A unique and remarkable novel" *La Croix*

"If there's an entry point into the work of the enduring, award-winning Italian writer Erri De Luca, then N.S. Thompson's excellent translation is surely it ... Thoughtful and wise about life and landscape, it's the most cerebral of whodunnits" *Observer*

"A morality-infused curio crisply translated by NS Thompson ... De Luca, a veteran author of some 70 books, explores the idea of the mountain as a dispassionate courtroom ... the inquiry – relayed as a transcript of questions and answers – peers into the chasm between knowledge and presumption" *Financial Times*

"Thought-provoking, philosophical ... De Lucca's *Impossible* is a wonderfully written and translated novella which makes you question the nature of justice, perception and reality" *BookBlast Diary*

Also by Erri De Luca in English translation

God's Mountain
The Day before Happiness
Three Horses
Me, You

ERRI DE LUCA

IMPOSSIBLE

Translated from the Italian by
N. S. Thompson

Copyright © Erri De Luca, 2019
This English-language edition published by
arrangement with Editions Gallimard, Paris

English translation copyright © N. S. Thompson, 2022

The moral right of Erri De Luca to be recognised as the author of this work has
been asserted in accordance with the Copyright, Designs and Patents Act, 1988

N. S. Thompson asserts his moral right to be identified
as the translator of the work

Originally published in Italian as *Impossibile* in 2019
by Giangiacomo Feltrinelli Editore, Milan
First published in the English language in 2022 by Mountain Leopard Press

This paperback edition published in 2024 by
Mountain Leopard Press
an imprint of
HEADLINE PUBLISHING GROUP

1

Apart from any use permitted under UK copyright law, this publication may
only be reproduced, stored, or transmitted, in any form, or by any means,
with prior permission in writing of the publishers or, in the case of
reprographic production, in accordance with the terms of licences
issued by the Copyright Licensing Agency.

All characters in this publication are fictitious and any resemblance
to real persons, living or dead, is purely coincidental.

Cataloguing in Publication Data is available from the British Library

ISBN (PB) 978 1 9144 9566 3

Designed and typeset in Scala by Libanus Press Ltd, Malborough
Printed and bound in Great Britain by Clays Ltd, Elcograf S.p.A.

Headline's policy is to use papers that are natural, renewable and recyclable
products and made from wood grown in well managed forests and other
controlled sources. The logging and manufacturing processes are expected
to conform to the environmental regulations of the country of origin

HEADLINE PUBLISHING GROUP
an Hachette UK Company
Carmelite House, 50 Victoria Embankment, London EC4Y 0DZ

www.headline.co.uk   www.hachette.co.uk

Often I heard tales of which I said, "Now this is a thing that cannot happen." But before a year had elapsed I heard that it actually had come to pass somewhere.

Isaac Bashevis Singer, *Gimpel the Fool*
TRANSLATED BY SAUL BELLOW

Q: Let's start again from the beginning of that day, shall we? You don't recognise the person in the photograph I've shown you?

A: No, I don't recognise him. I'm not good at faces and with good reason after so many years. I can only repeat what I've already said.

Q: Perhaps, but possibly you could add something you haven't said before?

A: Perhaps, but this isn't a friendly chat between passengers on a train. I'm being questioned by an examining magistrate in a pre-trial investigation. It's your decision what to ask, mine to decide if I want to talk about a memory or not.

Q: I can understand that. All the same, I must ask you to run over that day again.

A: I woke up early, around five o'clock. I waited till seven to go down to the dining hall for breakfast. Then I went to my room, brushed my teeth, went out to my car and drove off to the mountains. I'd decided to go for a hike up there. I chose a difficult route off the beaten track, so as not to meet other people. That day I chose the Cengia del Bandiàrac in the Val Badia. It's one of the most difficult and dangerous regions in the Dolomites.

So I left the car and set off along the official path from the Capanna Alpina up to the Col de Locia. At seven-thirty there was still no-one around so I was surprised to see someone higher up who'd started before me.

Q: And it was a man?

A: Yes, a man. In the mountains, people behave strangely. If you know there's someone behind you who's climbing up faster, you tend to increase your speed so as not to be overtaken. It's childish, but often happens. It's obvious that if the person below is faster, he'll catch up with the first. The one in front increases their pace, and soon they have to slow down or stop to catch their breath. Then there are those who pretend they have to tie a bootlace or stop to admire the view or take a photograph. If it's a couple, you hear the man telling the woman to hurry up and he'll say it in a loud voice to let you know he'd be much faster on his own.

If there's someone faster behind me, I slow down to let them pass. I don't like having anyone treading on my heels.

Q: You see, this aspect wasn't in your previous summary. You don't like having anyone behind you. You prefer to stay back and follow. That's interesting. Please go on.

A: I carried on as if to overtake him, but I didn't catch up with him. Evidently, I'd forced the pace. All the better. I prefer to be alone. When I go up at a steady pace, my body goes into a kind of state, while my mind wanders around between frivolous thoughts, serious ones, fantasies, snatches of song and conversations long past. Striding along is intense and I don't like to interrupt it to overtake someone and to have to say hello. When I'm out on a hike I never take a break. I'll slow down if I need to lower the pace, but I never stop.

The fact is I came to the end of the path at Col de Locia, where the high Fanes plateau starts, without having to overtake anyone. From there you leave the beaten track to proceed towards the Cengia del Bandiàrac, a slender ledge below the vertical wall of the Conturines peak, the highest in the Fanes group. It's a place known only to poachers in the past. And it annoyed me to see that figure striding along ahead of me towards it.

Q: He was hurrying?

A: From Col de Locia you first have to go down into a depression, then start climbing again. That man in front of me was actually running as he was going down. I went more slowly in the same direction. If he wanted to put some distance between us that was fine by me. I lost sight of him for a while, then spotted him again as he started on the Cengia path. He was a few hundred metres away as the crow flies.

Q: How long was it before you saw him again?

A: No more than a couple of hours. He was walking as if he were afraid.

Q: What do you mean "afraid"?

A: He was holding on to the rock wall. It's gravelly there, so you have to put the full weight of your body down as you step forward so as not to slip. But holding on to the rock wall makes it worse for the balance. It's the way people do who don't feel sure of their footholds.

Q: I understand. Please go on.

A: I thought no more about him. The route along that ledge requires concentration, looking down only at the ground step by step. It's as if you're trying to make no noise, because that would mean the scree was slipping from under your feet. On the Cengia del Bandiàrac you have to watch your step with that drop next to you.

I went on like this for about another hour, then came to a point where it looked as if there'd been a landslide. It happens. The rain and accumulated snow the previous winter can sweep away the path leaving a gap in the middle of it. I couldn't carry on. Had to turn back. I wasn't upset though; my aim had been to get out into the wilderness and I'd accomplished that.

The landslide wasn't recent, but you could see something at the bottom of it. I got out my binoculars and could see bits of clothing down among the rocks. It was impossible to get down there to check so I called the emergency services on 112 and reported it. I waited there to show the helicopter the spot. It arrived after about twenty minutes.

Then I turned back. And now several days later I'm repeating the day's events for the third time.

Q: So the two of you weren't together?

A: No, I go to the mountains to be alone. That man evidently did the same.

Q: You didn't hear him cry out? People usually do when they fall.

A: I didn't hear anyone cry out, otherwise I'd have hurried to try and help.

Q: What do you carry in your rucksack? Your binoculars and what else?

A: A length of rope and some carabiners in case I have to help someone in difficulty. A waterproof groundsheet and a thermal blanket in case I have to bivouac outside overnight. I don't carry any food or water.

Q: No compass?

A: I'm not out at sea.

Q: And you discovered later whose body that was?

A: From the news.

Q: A distinct surprise, I'd say. No? You were both on the same remote path forty years after the trial.

A: It was him or could have been anyone else. Accidents happen in the mountains. I've been lucky and avoided several.

Q: Accidents, yes. It's up to my office as investigating magistrate to establish whether or not this incident comes under the heading of an accident. The coincidence here arouses suspicion.

A: Coincidences happen all the time, many of them, and we don't even notice. But in this case, the word "coincidence" isn't enough for you?

Q: Between yourself and this man – who was once an informer, a collaborating witness, and helped the arrest of many of you, yourself included, with the result that you served a long prison sentence – I have to decide whether we're dealing with an accident or not and, in order to arrive at that, I need to exclude that the meeting was intentional.

A: So you're willing to call it an accident when a worker's been killed at work because he was pushed beyond the limits of endurance and those of the safety regulations? An accident is the term also used for the tens of thousands of injuries and the thousand deaths a year that manual workers get instead of their wages. And yet here you have doubts about the word when referring to a dangerous activity with risks freely taken on holiday with full responsibility taken for those risks.

That route along the Cengia is a difficult one. Did I take the man up there? Did I carry him on my shoulders in order to throw him off? Whoever goes up there takes that precipitous drop into account.

Your question should be this: who would make you do it with those conditions?

And the answer is no-one. We don't have an instigator here. There's no need, the mountain's enough for any motive. It's funny, isn't it, that something which doesn't move by itself could be seen as a motive force. But that's how it is; it draws things to itself. Everyone has their own motive for going there. Mine is so I can turn my back on everything and get away from it all. I chuck the whole world behind me. I place myself in empty space and an empty time. I see the world as it was and as it will be without us. A place that won't need to be left in peace.

Up there I'm a foreigner. No-one invites me and no-one welcomes me. Not even the war of a hundred years ago left a mark on those mountains. Any boulders detached by explosions rolled down as in any other time and left no sign.

A French alpinist called a book of his *Conquistadors of the Useless*. But that adjective "useless" means something to me. In the world of economics everything depends on the double entry system of credit and debit, on profit and usefulness. Well, going up into the mountains doesn't serve any purpose and doesn't want to: it's an effort of blessed uselessness.

I've been, and still am, a manual worker. It comes with certain dangers that go with the job, accounted for in the pay packet as danger money for the risks you take. In the mountains the risks are all my own, on holiday, free of any duties imposed on me, and perfectly useless.

What makes me do it? The beauty of the earth's crust that reaches out to its boundary with the air like a beach with the sea. To spend my energies up there needs no recompense.

Hah, dammit, when I start on about mountains I do let myself get carried away!

Q: You get me carried away too! I don't know anything about mountains and have little idea why people go there. May I ask you to continue?

A: If you think I allowed myself to go on there through tiredness and letting my defences down, you're mistaken. I've learned from my body when it's tired and to step up my attention and increase my lucidity. However, I've no wish to go over the events of that day yet again.

Q: We're proceeding well. You're explaining something interesting to an ignorant city dweller. Have you ever called that emergency number at any time before?

A: No, this was the first time.

Q: And this is the first time you've witnessed an accident in the mountains?

A: Alone, yes, in other cases the alarm had already been sounded.

Q: And how does it feel to witness a tragedy like that in the mountains?

A: Straightaway you try to understand how it happened, whether it was by error or something unforeseeable, overwhelming. You try to empathise. Then come the comments, the gossip about the killer mountain. But it's a wilderness, completely indifferent to us. It's not a sports ground or an amusement park. You don't need a pass to go there. You enter a land where no previous experience or equipment can guarantee you coming back safe and sound.

Q: And fear? I haven't heard you mention that.

A: Fear helps. It's a form of respect and even reverence owed to the size of the place you're travelling through. It seems vast, the more you go into it. Being afraid is a good basis for making you concentrate. It doesn't hinder your movement but increases your precision.

There are well-defined fears, they have a local habitation and a name. They demand recognition and decision-making.

It's a warning to the body that it's taking risks. On the Cengia del Bandiàrac hands are of no use, you go up and down along tiny strips of path barely outlined by the passage of chamois and next to sheer precipices.

But I'm talking about things that have to be experienced, they can't be explained.

And this interview has gone on long enough for me.

Q: I would ask you to continue with your account.

A: I can see that. But I do have the choice not to continue.

Q: Would you like to take a break? Have a coffee?

A: No thanks, I simply want to stop. Your technique of having me repeat things until I'm exhausted has achieved its aim. I'm indeed exhausted.

Q: It's your decision. For my part, given the circumstances of suspected murder disguised as an accident, I'm obliged in your case to place you in custody.

A: Then I'm under arrest?

Q: Judicial detention. You can designate a solicitor of your choice as your counsel, or one will be appointed to you by the prosecution.

Sweetheart, I'm thinking of that photo you sent me at Christmas of you as a child. That rascal face of yours looking directly into the lens, decisive, sarcastic, triumphantly defiant. I started to smile and the smile wouldn't leave my face. You were seven years old.

I don't know when you'll read this letter. For now I'm writing it to keep myself company with thoughts of the two of us being together.

The cell holding me for twenty-three hours a day is for solitary confinement, but I'm not isolating myself at all from you and what matters to me. I've lived in worse places. I have paper, a pen and time. I do gymnastics and go over everything I know by heart: songs, poems, proverbs.

I don't know exactly what I'm doing here, under what part of the Penal Code I'm being held. I'm entitled to a solicitor, but I don't want one and it wouldn't help me.

They'll foist one on me, some unlucky sod who can't refuse. With me he'll be able to do the least possible, I'll see to my own defence. A mistake to say defence, I'll see to my alienation.

The magistrate who is questioning me is half my age, knows nothing about mountains or the years of revolution. It should be me that's questioning him.

He's never been up a mountain and he's trying to find out why I go there.

I told him that we go there for nothing that serves any purpose, because the useless is beautiful. It's not an explanation, I know, but to ask a question about something you should know what you're asking about. I don't ask a pilot what flight is if I haven't been in an aeroplane.

I'm keeping back the best part of my reply for you. I go into the mountains because up there you come to the edge of the earth, its border with the sky, and all the universe is there above you. And so with a climb I can go on until there's nothing more to climb, I follow the earth as far as it was pushed up and continues to push upwards, because the mountains continue to grow.

I go to admire the forces up there that spend their limitless energy. This year I've crossed avalanches that have ripped up roads, forests knocked down by winds, mountainsides fallen into valleys. And, in the middle of these disasters, still animal life continues to exist and reproduce itself.

I come across chamois that run up slopes as if weightless, and lower down in the woods I can surprise the deer. These are creatures of sheer elegance, the effect of an intense surveillance of the dangers around them. Their vigilance is transformed into perfectly agile movement, their flight is a dance. I'm inspired by every encounter. If they stopped nearby I'd kneel down and kiss their hooves, as it were. It's crazy, but I'm not joking. They die at an early age before dragging life out, drained and exhausted.

I remember our days in the mountains here, you waking up complaining, following me around until breakfast at seven. Straightaway you came back to life, chatting with Erika. I'd put on two hardboiled eggs for you. Then we'd go out and you'd stop to photograph the clouds, flowers and tarns.

With you I learned the word love and the days were like Easter eggs, each one with a surprise inside.

Before meeting you I'd been in love before, but it was soon over. I fell out of love at the first disagreements.

With you I've learned a love that holds together and lasts beyond any argument, opposition or defect, until you love even those. It's love for your face when you're annoyed, when you explode and then, when you smile again.

And like in the mountains, I love every expression, even the rain and getting soaked while moving so the body isn't chilled and there's no need to shelter.

So I decided that my definition of love is you.

I call you Sweetheart, or Sweetie. You say it should be more than that, and that I should love you more. I don't know what this more is, or in what it consists.

I admit to not being enough for you.

At school I used to study, and applied myself, but my marks were less than average. My speciality was a five. The teacher would ask me questions and I found myself answering with less than I knew. Was it reticence or resistance? I didn't want to reply in full and kept back for me a part of what I should have answered. With you, on the other hand, I spill out everything and I know it's not enough for you.

With this magistrate, it's like being asked questions back in school. Only the ages are upside down: I'm the ancient pupil in the remedial class, he's the young supply teacher who knows less about the subject than I do.

With him I'm back to my old reticence.

With you I give everything and can see it's not enough. But I'm rambling. I can't talk about love for more than five minutes, so you protest, and the smile at the beginning of this letter comes back. I'll close it with you sulkily reproaching me.

Sweetheart, another letter from me, seeing as I'm stuck in here. You might think that being in solitary means silence. On the contrary, the row of cells here is full of noise, echoing with cries and clanks of metal.

This afternoon I imagined I was in a sailing boat out at sea. The daylight hours were shortening, the air cooler, the direction north. Days without wind, no movement in latitude or longitude, days skewered stiff as if by a butterfly collector. I was familiar with them from my purgatory days. Today was one of those days. I refused to go out into the exercise yard for a breath of air. So I stayed in my cabin and gazed at the maps on the ceiling.

I'm not worried about this trip, where and when it'll come into dock on dry land. What matters to me is that the days have direction, with a prow that slowly moves forward with time. I don't peep out through a porthole at an endless low tide, nothing to see or measure.

Days come back to me when I was shut in a cell with prisoners who tried to turn them into pieds-à-terre. Then the searches turned them upside down and back into cells. Solitary is better. There's nothing to gather up nor put back in place. Here inside you forget about being a body in this world.

There's a pile of reasons to stop believing in things, here inside. I get by in not believing in the cell.

The magistrate let me know he's not going to summon me. Nice of him. He could have kept me in suspense. But I'm not waiting for anything. I'm here and that's it and I'm trying to get used to it. The aim isn't freedom but getting over the first week. Once you get over the start, then how much more doesn't matter. It's like at the beginning in a factory; the machines go round, they move, and a worker has to fit in with the system until he's a part of it. At various times of the day I forget where I am. It's the first sign of adaptation.

The magistrate is from the south, same as me, but I can't tell where from his accent. He could be from Abruzzo or Molise. He's a long dark streak and stares at me with sharp, penetrating eyes, like in photographs of your grandparents once upon a time. I stare back at him.

It's the only thing I can do as a man accused to be on a level with him. When he realises I'm scrutinising him he starts shuffling his papers. His eyelids are reddish and his thick eyebrows are like two moustaches. He wears glasses and often takes them off to show that he's a willing listener. He wants to give me enough rope. If he thinks I'm going to hang myself he's wasting his time. If he thinks I'm going to trip myself up with some discrepancy when talking, he's got the wrong man. I can't trip myself up because if you do that in the mountains you fall off.

He suspects that I pushed that guy off the ledge on the Cengia. I know you're not interested in whether I'm guilty or not. You wanted me as I was when we met, not bothering about my past. You asked me nothing about those years of conflict and public rage. I'm grateful for your willingness to let the past start with the two of us. You weren't interested in who I was before you entered my life. You wouldn't leave me even if I was declared guilty. We talked about it once in the abstract – if I had to go to prison you wouldn't visit me and you wouldn't write, but you would wait. We shook hands to seal the deal.

What matters to you is the two of us, only us two. The

rest of the world is out of focus, you have to put on glasses to see it. You live a long way away in that place beyond the medians, but I've trained myself to talk to you like this. Here, inside, I talk out loud to myself to let you know what I'm doing and what's passing through my head.

For me, freedom isn't being able to walk about outside, it's in putting words together for you and what they mean. I tell you that I care deeply for you, and I do it all the time. Freedom is in keeping ourselves together even with me inside. No prison cell can take that freedom away.

I've no grudge against the magistrate. He's attempting a Socratic dialogue with me, hoping this will bring the truth to light. Perhaps he's thinking of his studies and the art of dialectics.

And if he thinks the truth's nestling inside me and he's looking to be the midwife to give it birth, he'll have to realise the womb is empty!

And with that very poor play on words, I'll end this letter. Till the next one, Sweetie.

Q: We are resuming the interview in the presence of a solicitor to act as counsel appointed by the Prosecutor's Office because you haven't appointed one yourself.

Now, you knew the man who fell from the Cengia del Bandiàrac because, as an informer, he reported you many years ago.

A: I don't recognise the term informer.

Q: A witness for the State in a prosecution. What definition would you use?

A: A person who informs on his own comrades in order to gain a reduction of sentence, or his freedom, I would call a traitor.

Q: What if one were dealing with a deeply thought-out repentance? He no longer shared the movement's political line and gave himself over to a course of self-criticism. Of his own free will.

Informing on his own comrades was an act of liberation that could favour whoever was still in a blind alley and offer them a way out. I've met several people from your movement who admitted they were saved from worse by getting arrested. Don't you think such a course of reflection is more human and shows greater complexity than can be described by the verb betray?

A: Whoever informs on his own comrades comes within the definition of the verb betray. What you call repentance is a denial, a renunciation, prompted by the several advantages of the witness protection programme, from a change of name to a return to freedom.

Repentance is something interior and doesn't sell itself. It's to do with an individual's conscience and not judicial proceedings.

You can imagine that I've had time to consider this for longer than you and well before you.

Q: So you're a diehard, unrepentant?

A: Unrepentant about what? Because I don't deny who I am or beat my chest like a penitent? The penitentiary saw to beating it for me and reducing me to the role of detainee for many years.

I paid my debt without any reduction. The sentence given was unrepentant, even for a day.

I reject your definition that claims to judge the opinion I have of my political struggle.

Q: An unrepentant in our current speech is someone who still considers legitimate the crime they committed. It's synonymous with irrecoverable, if you prefer.

A: This is your language, that of those for whom the sentence served is never long enough. The punishment serves to pay the debt to society and settle the account with the State, but you want us to be debtors for life. You are the diehards, the unrepentant ones who want a continual rejection of the past way beyond the bars of a cell.

Q: That's rich, you still put things the wrong way round. You no longer fight with weapons, but with words.

I can see that you are fixed solidly in the past, with an absolute want of self-criticism.

A: Once upon a time we ourselves engaged in debates and critiques about the past. We produced books and critical papers. But here, between us, with you who accuses and me who refutes the accusation, self-criticism's out of place. Here self-criticism would be a *mea culpa* and a request for mitigating circumstances. Between you and me there's no mitigation. You're keeping me in prison, and I have to put up with it. Furthermore, because of your age, you weren't around to witness what was going on in those days and I don't take you seriously as someone who can talk about events in those days.

Solicitor: As your solicitor I would advise you to keep to a more measured tone of voice and to topics within the scope of the accusation. I suggest we try to dismantle the accusation on the basis of the evidence alone.

A: Thank you, but you are not my solicitor and I don't need one. You're here because legal procedure requires it. So I would ask you not to interfere.

Solicitor: Are you asking me not to perform my role?

A: As far as my case is concerned, yes.

Q: Gentlemen, you can discuss this elsewhere. May we continue?
   Why would a course of self-criticism be a request for mitigating circumstances?

A: Following the course of the Prodigal Son who comes home as a penitent to be readmitted to the family. I'm here before you under an accusation, not as a penitent, so I'll keep my self-criticism to myself.

Q: It's true I couldn't be your age in those years, but I am informed about the trials. Do you still consider that person an enemy of yours?

A: Knowing the events of an era by means of judicial proceedings is like studying the stars by looking at their reflection in a pond.

You use the word enemy. There was a time in this country when my political generation was regarded as a public enemy. There was a magistracy that dedicated itself exclusively to our repression. They calmly used the term struggle. They sat in the judgment seat and continued to be enemies. But there's no personal animosity here at all. There was a public involved and we entered back into that public.

Q: I'm asking you again if that person who fell from the Cengia del Bandiàrac was your enemy?

A: That era's been over for decades, as have the consequences that we served in prison, so any feelings of hostility have long been extinguished. My feelings and my politics remain the same, however, but I no longer have enemies. The time of enemies is locked away in the last century.

Q: What do you think about the man who informed on you?

A: An outsider, someone who wanted out of our community. I stopped caring about him half a lifetime ago.

Q: What do you think about the fact that you were both on the same path on the same day at the same time?

A: A coincidence.

Q: That, for me, is an incomplete definition. Was this an intentional coincidence or simply fortuitous? For me as an investigator, a coincidence is evidence. If we apply a numerical value to the probability, it would be nought point several other noughts. So, I have to look for another explanation. For the two of you to have been there by chance is so improbable as to be impossible.

A: Impossible is only a definition of an event until it happens. With all the noughts you want, you and statistics can't deny the fact of coincidence. They happen despite all your noughts. A number of discoveries testify to that effect, and a number of disasters too. A person walks across a bridge the moment it collapses. Many other people walked over it just before. Instead of being rare, coincidences are a constant. That that man and I should happen to be a few hundred metres apart in that deserted place at the very same time is for me today a clear and unshakable case. From the point of view of a witness present at the scene I know that the impossible actually happened.

Q: We'll come back to the hundreds of metres' distance. Here we're not talking about the fortuitous case of two men who meet and we don't know how. We're talking about the consequence of this meeting, one of the two of you having fallen.

A: Meeting, you say? I'd rule out the idea of a meeting. I saw a man from a distance. I witnessed the fact that he had fallen. I called 112. That's how you know I was there. I could have walked by, not reported it and I wouldn't be here having to talk about it. But in the mountains you have to come to people's aid. He could have been still alive and prompt action could save time. I did my duty and it's been turned into an accusation of murder.

Q: Even your phone call is capable of an alternative interpretation. Having identified the body and your previous history, we would have checked the guest lists in the accommodation down in the valley. We would have found his name. With that phone call, you tried to put yourself beyond suspicion. You know, besides, that you're easily identified. You're about the only person who wears sandals in the mountains. Any witness would remember having seen you that day and at that time on that route that leads to the Col de Locia.

By the way, why do you wear sandals?

A: Is it important?

Q: I think it may be.

A: Well, alright. They're not sandals for the beach, but for hiking. They're technically designed for it, and for supporting the foot. I started using them because going downhill in boots with laces puts pressure on my toenails and they began to fall out. It doesn't happen anymore with these heavy-duty hiking sandals. They also have the advantage of strengthening the foot and stop you twisting your ankle, which remains separate from the sandal and not involved in the twisting that rocky ground provokes. Over the rocks I tighten the adjustable straps and can even climb in them.

Q: So you don't slip in them?

A: That depends entirely on how you place your foot on a slope.

Q: I'm not sure I follow you exactly. Let's go back to your 112 call. Why did you make that call? To be one step ahead before being identified and questioned. And for another reason. It was a challenge to let us know you were there. Declaring your presence was half of the revenge: revenge disguised as an accident.

Allow me to quote some lines from Racine's *Phèdre*:

> *Ma vengeance est perdue*
> *s'il ignore en mourant*
> *que c'est moi qui le tue.*

"My vengeance is lost if he's ignorant when dying that it is I who is killing him."

You wanted both him and us to know. With that telephone call you satisfied both wishes.

A: You've admitted knowing nothing about mountains. If that man had been running any risk, I would have helped him, even if I'd known who he was. That's how it is and how it has to be. There are no friends or enemies when someone's in trouble and needs help. You don't even know the geography there.

Q: I'll enquire about the possibility of a visit. Today there are means of surveying from a distance with drones.

A: That may be enough to make observations on a little monitor. It won't help you to know how it is at that very point. This is how you collect evidence in your day, with C.C.T.V. and D.N.A. But how you look for the truth of facts at the scene is a lost art. You can send a drone to the top of Mount Everest, but don't tell me that's enough and it wouldn't have been useful to have been up there.

Q: And how was evidence collected in your day? It was down to fingerprints, that's all.

A: In my day all you people had to do was listen to a traitor and you made mass arrests without any reaction in the press.

Q: Let's leave that. I can begin to believe you that facing an emergency sets off the instinct to offer first aid. Except there's no emergency here. There are two of you on that crumbling ledge of the Cengia. And one of you throws the other off, after having followed and caught up with him. If there was a struggle, the traces would be swept away by the wind.

Looking at the actual facts, the only explanation of what you term a coincidence is in fact premeditated murder. A motive exists and I intend to prove it. You may consult with your appointed solicitor, who is an able and conscientious professional.

A: I don't need one. This is a matter between you as a representative of the State and myself. I'm an old man now and I've seen a great deal. I'm not worried about this situation. I have no wife or children waiting for me at home and ashamed about the added murder charge.

It seems strange to tell you I'm an old man, when I actually have more time than you. Not only the time already past, but also that now. I have time in that cell. I use it to think ahead of you. You traipse behind me, as if forced to follow me into the mountains. Let's go to a tribunal, to trial. It's the right place for a citizen who finds himself up against the State. Here in this pre-trial inquiry we're still in the changing rooms before the match.

You can take away my freedom of movement, but not the freedom of my thoughts and convictions.

Q: I would argue with you about this being a matter between you and me. There's nothing personal here. I represent the Public Prosecution Service and am carrying out this investigation because it's my job.

A: I know, but for me you are the State, and I'm facing a personal question, one on one with the establishment. And this solicitor appointed by you to defend me...

Q: Please don't confuse the roles here. The solicitor is appointed by the Public Prosecution's office, not by me.

A: If the solicitor has the least interest in defending me, he can put forward an application for bail and provisional liberty.

Solicitor: I'll certainly look into the possibility.

Sweetheart, I'm well and even the hospital diet here is fine for a locked space. I chat with you continually, more than when we're together and you tell me off for not talking enough. You'd be surprised how much I do talk to you in here.

I once read a witty piece by a female American writer who admitted talking to herself, explaining it by saying she appreciated the good listener and an intelligent conversation. It's not exactly like that in here. I'm describing a bunch of things, whatever, from the cockroaches to the bolts on the doors.

And in the meantime, my hearing's improved. Talking about cockroaches, I can hear them running around at night like bison on the plains. When there's profound silence, the ears open up in search of sounds. I can hear the night guard's teaspoon stirring in his cup beyond the doors to our row of cells.

As soon as the sound of voices and jangling metal starts up, a shutter closes in my ears and I'm deaf again.

You depend on your hearing inside, the other senses lag behind.

I can sense it on my skin a little that the air around me changes in density and temperature when you come to me. My wrist becomes the second home of my heartbeat. I put my thumb on it to feel it skipping a beat on your arrival.

In these days the scirocco beats against all surfaces. Last night I could hear swirls of dust brushing against the walls. I had strange thoughts: what direction did they go round in, clockwise or anti-clockwise? Did you know that cyclones move differently depending on which hemisphere they're in? I don't remember which direction they go in ours.

I tried to understand by the brushing sound. Strange thoughts, but worthwhile. They keep me company and entertain me. When they stop, I smile about them.

The dialogue with the young magistrate is going well. He's now looking for proof with a drone, playing around with it and the hypothesis he wants to put forward. I'm his adversary.

He quoted me some lines from Racine I happen to know, about vengeance. He tried to impress me on the cultural level because he knows I didn't go to university. But I've certainly read more than he has.

I find I've a lot of useful spare time here inside. I once told you that I've never been bored in my life, not even for a minute. Boredom is time wasted and I avoid it. A writer once wrote a novel about it. I've not read it, not even out of curiosity for what it says.

You ask me how I spend my time. Don't laugh if I tell you. I keep myself busy. Doing what? Besides physical exercises, which I turn into a challenge, I work at puzzles.

I'm fascinated by palindromes, words that can be read forwards and backwards. I made one up against a missile launcher: I did live, evil did I. That's for what they do against cities, houses and gardens. The cowardice of modern warfare.

I also occupy myself with anagrams. Here's one that reflects me. Solitary: Lo, I stay.

I concentrate all day, so by the evening I'm tired. Yes, I can concentrate inside. I even came up with a rhyme.

The poems I know by heart I can tell myself for company. There's one I remember in particular. I was at the dinner table with a family whose daughter I was in love with – we were just kids at secondary school.

The father was studying me a little suspiciously, but in a well-meaning way with the hint of an ironic smile. He asked me about schoolwork, and I complained that they loaded us up with poems to learn by heart. I couldn't imagine then how useful they'd be in prison.

He wanted to know which ones, for example. Obviously, there were excerpts from Dante's "Divine Comedy", but also individual poems and he wanted to test me to see if it was all true. In the sudden silence I could feel my memory giving way. I should have recited the story of Ulysses in the "Inferno", but all that came to mind was a sonnet to Beatrice in the *Vita Nuova*. We took the mickey out of it in class because it was a bit soppy for us adolescent boys.

So I had to translate it from our burlesque performance into something serious. The girl I was in love with was staring at me, along with the rest of the table. I should have returned the stare and dedicated the sonnet to her. Instead, I looked directly at the father who was opposite me. I cleared my voice and spelled out each syllable. Then I pronounced the last word "Sigh!" in anger, interpreting it as a condemnation of desiring a love in vain, without any hope of it being reciprocated, rather than a word coming from Beatrice's sweet soul.

Sigh: I often say it to myself these days and I'm pleased I didn't dedicate it to anyone before you. And I've learned to say the last syllable as it should be said.

I'm sleeping soundly, even though at night now there's an addict in withdrawal in our solitary row. While the poor man was raving until he could barely croak, thoughts of you came to me as if they were your letters:

> Going out to an aquarium when we wanted to see dolphins, then seeing them swimming near your house.
> Sitting on the sofa with a glass of cold beer, watching films on your enormous screen.
> You sulking when you lose at cards, and being rude when you win.
> The trick you played on me when I was reversing and you banged the door to make me think I'd hit something.

> The days when we do as you do with a pig, throwing nothing away.
>
> When I'm doing my exercises, twisting my head from side to side, and you ask me if I love you. I say "Yes", but I'm still shaking my head from side to side, so you say, "Well, make your mind up!"

In here you're everywhere. I didn't imagine you could be here constantly. Certainly, it's me who's thinking of you, but it's you who comes alive and looks after me with your presence until it's time for bed.

With you in here I don't know what being far away is any more.

I imagine the woods behind Erika's house, early morning, sun filtering through the needles on the pine trees, droplets glistening and trembling on them. I stand up by the wall and begin my exercises. I carry on for about an hour, rest for two, then have another hour. Every so often I get an idiotic thought about a heart attack while I'm keeping fit in here. But my heart still keeps pumping the blood round till I feel it in my ears and its singing reassures me. I must at least get to the end of this dialogue with the State. Both my heart and I are curious as to how it will pan out.

And so this letter ends with wishing you a good day, Sweetheart.

Q: Let's pick up on those questions again. And your solicitor is here. How are you?

A: I'm well, but not the young chap going through withdrawal in the cell nearby. He's not even been given any medication and he's yelling all night.

Q: He has to be in solitary or they'd beat him to death in the other cells to make him keep quiet.

A: A sensitive concern on your part. He goes through withdrawal and if he doesn't kill himself first, then he'll survive.

Q: Leaving that aside, have you reflected on your position, the extreme coincidence that places the two of you on that same route? Have you considered the unlikelihood? Do you maintain it was simply fortuitous?

A: I've no other explanation. I also want to say that I've no intention of paying this solicitor. He hasn't even applied for bail.

Solicitor: There's no point at the moment; it would be refused.

Q: We have a witness that morning who saw you walking up the route from the Capanna Alpina to the Col de Locia. He remembers your lean figure and your hiking sandals. He also remembers you walking without trekking poles. Don't you use them, or was it just that day you didn't want them?

A: I don't use them. The body bent forward is the wrong position for going upwards. Your witness repeats what I've already said, and you already know. I was on that route and then on to the Cengia.

Q: We need independent confirmation of your testimony. Did you know that you were following that person?

A: I knew that there was someone in front of me.

Q: In fact, you were following him.

A: In fact, no. In fact, there was someone ahead of me along a stretch that was the only possible route. I go to the mountains to be alone.

Q: The post-mortem is being carried out and a forensic examination of the victim's clothing. If you have left any traces on those garments you will have to tell me how they came to be there. Wouldn't it be better to anticipate the results and lighten your position somewhat? By collaborating and admitting to a close encounter you would avail yourself of various benefits. Moreover, it would relieve you of the weight that must certainly be pressing on your conscience.

A: Informing on myself would be a novel experience, certainly.

Solicitor: I'm obliged to add that, in effect, one's legal position is greatly improved if an admission of guilt is given before the forensic evidence is known.

A: I've no need of your advice, thank you. For me, you are an intruder on this debate, and I must ask you not to intervene.

Q: How did you succeed in making him fall? You were both in a precarious position and you could easily have fallen yourself.

A: Why don't you tell me, seeing as you believe you already know. I don't know how he fell. What I do know is that the Cengia is a narrow, crumbling shelf exposed to the elements.

Q: I think I do know, but it would be helpful to have your version of events, either to correspond with mine or to refute it. I believe you were following that man, you caught up with him and caused him to panic and fall to his death.

A: I refuse to go along with this fantasy of yours. Would it help you if I were guilty? I'll see you in court.

Solicitor: I would advise you at least to think twice about the tone of your responses.

A: Excuse me, you are far too young to be giving me advice. I've passed so much more of my life than you facing precipices to be worried by this balcony on the first floor.

Solicitor: You're prejudiced against me. You think I'm on the prosecution's side, whereas my duty is to be on yours.

A: Please leave us. I'll think about my own case. Alone.

Q: We'll resume this interview when the forensic reports are in. In the meantime, you will remain at the disposition of the judicial authorities.

A: And still no request for bail from my supposed solicitor here to defend me? I know that people are held in custody if there's a danger a crime may be repeated, evidence tampered with or the person absconding.

Solicitor: You are well informed. Indeed, the danger of your absconding is enough for a magistrate to keep you in custody, in view of your rebellious nature in the past.

A: Congratulations, you anticipate the motives for the refusal of a request you haven't made and don't intend to make.

Solicitor: You can always nominate a solicitor of your own choosing and relieve me of the role.

Q: This interview is now suspended.

Here I am, Sweetheart, back in my few metres under lock and key. It's raining outside, I can hear it pattering in the guttering. You didn't study Latin, unlike me. In it, there are two verbs for "to ask". One means to ask in order to know something, the other is used to ask to obtain something.

The magistrate was continuing with his questions, wanting to know the truth. That's not true. He was asking because he wants to obtain confirmation of what he thinks he already knows. He doesn't use the verb of curiosity of someone who wants information or wants to know a truth directly. He doesn't need to.

I remembered these two verbs while he was questioning me.

My solicitor pretended to be on my side of the table, while in fact he's with the prosecution. He doesn't even want to put in a request for bail.

They want me to confess to having followed this man and then thrown him off the cliff. You should have heard my solicitor recommending the advantages of a confession. It would have been like watching a theatrical performance. They've no proof and they want me to hand it to them.

Outside the days are turning autumnal and I can feel my body slowing down. We have a friendly climate that allows us to slide gently into winter and its reduced light. The first woollens put the body into isolation.

We've cared for each other deeply for ten years. For me you're the same woman for whom I carried a suitcase that first day, when we happily used the second person "tu" directly, without passing through that false pretence of the third person "lei" first.

By the way, thinking of that first time leads me to the second. It was confirmation of our meeting and the intention to find ourselves together and continue the relationship. From that moment on, all our times have been that second time, getting better and more intimate.

You can't stand being tickled and I don't inflict it on you. Your feet are cold in winter and I warm them for you. In summer I'm on the watch for mosquitoes so they don't come near you. You smile when I examine your legs and arms to beat off any intruders. In exchange you advise me on spices and shoes and trim the hair in my ears. Our relationship's built on this attentiveness. Elegance is in the consideration two people show each other as a couple, rather than in the clothes they wear.

We're still at the second stage and stopped counting.

My hands are useless when I look at them, empty with no tools.

I think about yours with no nail polish, ready to work with anything from needle to hammer. You like broad beans, so I plant them for you. Your garden's yellow with lemons, and no weeds. You don't throw anything away – stones of fruit and olives, ruined tomatoes – you put them back in the ground on the chance they'll grow again. These are the good things you do by nature, without even thinking about it. I think I'm at fault having kept you all this time. If you've grown a wrinkle, or let yourself go, then the fault's mine. It's my fault I can't arrest your time while I'm under arrest and incapable of stopping the course of yours. I'm playing with words, I know. But it's a pain right in the middle of the forehead. It's my fault for having kept you so long. To make it worse, I'll add that it isn't enough, and I want to stay with you for the rest of my life.

Certainly, you were and still are free to break things off, but you in turn have persisted in having me. You're holding onto me even now. Between us the words holding onto each other are the right ones.

In your good moments I can make you laugh, but when you're sad I can't budge you from that sadness.

I love it when you're on the telephone, still sleepy, I can hear you yawning because you haven't had your coffee. For me that's impossible, I have to put the coffee pot on first thing. Here I have to learn to do without. It's fine to experiment doing without things that don't matter much, like doing without coffee when you wake up.

Instead, I do stretch exercises with my fingers on the security door. There's a notch in the iron fixtures I can hang from.

I'm learning to make a friend of time. I present myself as the same age. Time's forever and so am I, even if my forever is shorter. We live together in the same minutes; space doesn't matter; we can have our immensities within the centimetres of the cell. You are also here and that's all that matters to me.

Before you, when faced with a woman, I couldn't allow myself to think of a relationship. There were unions in the years of revolution, rather than love. Then came a long abstinence and then, back in the world, it was obvious I couldn't offer a decent future to any woman.

Then you came along, and the reticence and uncertainty vanished. You turned things upside down, the formulae with which I used to justify my missing out. Your presence put my days one behind the other in Indian file, moving towards our appointed meetings.

Who knows why I'm able to write to you inside these sealed-off walls things I could never say out loud. Perhaps it's the emptiness around me that helps. It's different from up in the mountains where things keep churning inside you as you climb. Here the emptiness keeps me still.

Detainees take care in their letters not to show too much nostalgia for things. Seeing as I don't suffer from it, I do the opposite and emphasise my affectionate side.

From the moment I was in here I immediately oriented myself to the cardinal points. The solitary cells are in the north wing, the door is to the south, so I turn my back on it and the west is on my left. At the end of every day I look west, knowing you're somewhere in that direction. That's the wonder of everyday thought. Don't explain it to me, it's a gift from you, without any reason or my deserving it. It's your perfect gift.

Now we come to a delicate matter. Sometimes you ask me if I'm jealous. And I say no, because I love you. The word love changes everything. If you take it away you're left with nothing. It's then you become jealous. So I hang on to the word love. It's precious.

In my other time in prison, a cellmate would despair thinking his wife or girlfriend might find someone else. They'd be exasperated by the time of the monthly visit and came back to the cell even worse. I didn't understand them. What were those women to do, the grass widows? I tried consoling but only made it worse. One man said to me, "What are we, nothing but spare parts that can be replaced?"

I should have said yes, we were replaceable, but didn't.

And that's how it is, Sweetheart, when you're dealing with long separation, prison or emigration. It's better to leave it to time and not sworn oaths.

You're a woman in the fullness of life. You feel an

overwhelming desire for a man? Then express it and act on it. I hope you don't fall in love, but even if you do I'll still love you. The happiness you may get from someone else takes nothing away from you for me. It's a happiness you couldn't get from me.

With you I have a whole bag of assorted happinesses, you haven't made me miss a single one; instead, you've invented some I couldn't have imagined of you. They're specifically mine and couldn't be repeated with anyone else.

That's how things are with regard to happiness.

Q: We resume the interview. The accused's solicitor is present. The forensic evidence still isn't in, but I deem it right to attempt one last interview without it.

You were many years in a youthful protest movement.

A: It was a revolutionary movement, not a student protest.

Q: Can you help me with the terms here? You were a full-time militant, as it used to be defined then, an adherent who dedicated himself completely to political activism. Would that be correct?

A: Yes, I was a militant, full-time, maintained by the movement.

Q: The years of your youth were employed in this activity?

A: All the years of my youth, from eighteen to thirty.

Q: It's evident that such dedication brings with it an ideal and practical belief that renders those years the most important in your life.

A: Certainly the most full and communal, but I wouldn't be able to judge how important they were.

Q: Unlike other militants from that time, you've remained faithful and attached to that period, untroubled by any feelings of remorse. Others have openly distanced themselves, even repudiating their actions and without any aim to gain thereby from the judicial system.

A: They distanced themselves from themselves.

Q: Help me here. Your feelings towards them are those of contempt, given the terms you use?

A: I couldn't socialise with them, but I don't feel anything as painful as contempt.

Q: So, your feelings would be stronger towards someone who had collaborated with the State you were fighting, who informed on you and had your comrades arrested. Here your feelings are total aversion, hate, rancour, a spirit of revenge. Am I going too far?

A: Not too far, simply wrong. Before I go on, though, may I forgo the physical presence of my solicitor? It's nothing personal, just that I prefer to talk man to man.

Q: I'm afraid such a request cannot be entertained. The absence of a solicitor during an interview with someone accused is inconceivable and unconstitutional.

A: Then I won't continue. I can't get over a presence that is superfluous and even obstructive.

Solicitor: I'm not allowed out of this room, but I don't have to sit next to you. I can arrange myself behind you, moving my chair closer to the door.

A: I thank you for your consideration. In that case we can proceed.

Q: Unorthodox, but I'm happy with it.

A: Then I'll continue. Whoever betrays anyone betrays themselves. However much they convince themselves of having done the right thing, they've cut a part of themselves away, their youth. I know of an efficient traitor who led the Carabiniere to where they could arrest his comrades. He asked that they be treated well at the time of arrest, because they were the best people he'd ever known. He knew they'd be tortured, but even while betraying them he continued to admire them.

These people know they degrade themselves. They carry a burden of disgrace. I've no hate, rancour or spirit of revenge. Decades have passed, popes have died, Olympic games passed and gone, the world's been turned inside out like a glove. That twentieth century is so long passed as to be incomprehensible to anyone coming after. If I had the feelings you attribute me, I'd be a sick man.

You accuse me of hate. I want to tell you something. You know the charges that led me to being bundled from prison to prison on islands small and large. I was also condemned for armed robbery to finance the movement. The man who informed on me and the others admitted he'd also taken part. He testified that never a shot had been fired.

On one of these bank raids, there was a little boy with his mother. Robbers storming in frightened him and he began to cry. One of them went up to him and said we were only playing, that this was a joke. He showed him his pistol and squeezed the trigger that went click on an empty chamber. He'd taken the cartridge out and the magazine. The little kid calmed down and smiled. The robbery was over and they made off with what they'd raked out of the tills.

Have you worked out who the robber was who calmed the little boy down? The man on the Cengia.

Another time we were being chased, running away on foot. All of a sudden he stops, while I continue running. He stops and threatens to throw a hand grenade at the squad car. It goes into reverse and is off. It was no hand grenade but a banana painted grey. The bomb was phoney, but he wasn't. You ask if I hate this man. Whoever passes the days of years like that doesn't change their ideas like clothes for the season. You remain stuck inside them.

Q: Do you have any other memories of this man? When you were together, that is.

A: He used to read Jack London, not the political texts common among us militants. He said London was a revolutionary, writing his stories from the right perspective. At the beginning of the twentieth century, he said the revolution was already here.

He preferred *The Star Rover* out of all his works. One night, out in the open, he told me that the name "star" was wrong. He called them "earths". I told him call them what you like, they don't matter to us, we have to take care of this world and leave astronomers to worry about the stars. All those shimmering stars put me to sleep.

Anyway, that's how he was, in his own way. Every one of us was, but from serried ranks we were uniform inside. Even if he was invisible – he took himself off. He was bored with political discussions. But when it mattered, he behaved well.

I wouldn't have expected him to betray us, not him, no.

Q: From the trial transcripts of your movement, we can reconstruct your career in it. You and this man formed part of the armed brigade.

A: It wasn't only the two of us, we were a small band that all came together at the same moment.

Q: Did you know each other before this?

A: From school, we were in the same student group.

Q: So, you grew up together, you knew each other well.

A: In so far as you can know each other, holding the same ideas and putting them into practice as a follow-up. I'm referring to the sharing of money, lodgings, food, cleaning. Equality also comes into the domestic sphere. We knew each other's habits, but almost nothing about someone's private life.

We had one odd thing in common, though, we liked tennis rather than football. He'd actually played it, I hadn't. He managed to get tickets for the international tournament in Rome, the best seats, in the grandstand.

We dressed up for it. I liked the doubles, he preferred the singles.

While I was watching he took advantage of people's attention on the game to lift several wallets from their pockets. He wasn't stealing for himself; it went into the common kitty. He was the opposite of me. While I was enjoying the rallies of the top players, he wouldn't let himself enjoy some time off. A tennis tournament had to be some use as well.

He was light-fingered, he lifted my wallet without my realising it. He did it for practice, but said it was too easy to relieve me of it. I couldn't even steal a book from a shelf.

Q: And yet you were sentenced for armed robbery.

A: To finance the movement. If I had had to do it for myself, I would have backed out. Theft paralyses me. Stretching out my hand to take something from somebody is impossible for me. Our programme was the opposite: stretching out the hand to give everyone a rightful share.

I used to tell him he was a thief and showed no respect for the tennis he liked.

"It's a game only for the rich," he told me. "I like it, but it's a throwback to my bourgeois roots. So I counterbalance it with something useful to the cause."

And he said, "It's a tax on contributors in arrears. I'm not a thief but a revenue collector."

He wanted to strip the clothes from the well off.

I didn't have the same family scruples, my father was a tram driver, my mother a cleaner, paid by the hour. We lived out in a village; a life of ease was never a reality for us.

The bourgeoisie helped him later, he was defended by a famous barrister and he sang out his whole recantation.

Q: So, the class difference mattered in your relationship, a complex mixture of admiration, challenge and action.

A: You can listen to all this, but you don't really understand. You have to form judgments and give out verdicts, but what do you know of what we held together and shared out together?

Q: Did the sharing out also extend to your relations with women?

A: Above all, we were comrades-in-arms. And I'm not giving way to chitchat. Can we stick to the crime page rather than the gossip column?

Q: This isn't a matter of gossip or who was going with whom. I'm trying to find out if there were any disagreements between you on the romantic level.

A: Are you now shifting your search for a motive towards a crime of passion? This is ridiculous.

Q: I withdraw the question. The fact remains, you weren't in monastic orders, there were women there. I refer to your comrades in the movement. Emotional ties were created and broken.

A: The reason for which we were together prevailed above all else, and we decided the final outcomes of our lives.

Q: And those of others? This time I'm not referring to the people killed. What about the lives of your parents, brothers, sisters, even children? You forced them to follow you around from prison to prison all over Italy to be near you.

A: I won't allow you to talk about them.

Q: I will withdraw the observation.

But I thank you for all these details. They make the picture and the motive more complex. In order to keep to the hypothesis of an attack on the Cengia I need to look again at the dynamics involved. For you the man wasn't a simple traitor. This was a man with whom you shared the intense bond of those who trust one another. A man you also admired. There's even the gratitude for an action that allowed you to escape arrest.

I have to understand that for you, vengeance is something more agonising than a violent settling of scores over time. You had to strip away deep feelings, stuck there, as you've said. It needed years in gaol for you to tear away the emotion in your feelings. And when that man was long buried for you, that's when he came back. So it's the past that throws things up, and they're not past if a chance encounter's enough to cause a nervous reaction.

If you had ever prayed in your life, it would have

been never to meet him again. If such a prayer were ever sent to heaven, it was not heard.

I'm trying to empathise with the kind of person I believe you are, in order to fill the space you leave empty. One gets fragments of discourse from you – with gaps in the middle – that I have to piece together. A motive can be assigned to a crime, but how many previous motives go to make it?

Are you familiar with the myth of Theseus in the labyrinth? My investigation isn't getting to the Minotaur but finding the passageways that led to it. The Minotaur is merely a formality.

A: Like a peak at the end of a climb.

Q: Exactly. You feel isolated in today's time and society. You go into the mountains to take advantage of the space there and the distance from others. You would be a type of lay hermit and retreat into the wilderness so as not to share the present.

But your past has remained untouched, and nothing stops a hermit from committing a crime. Alright, you feel no hate. This means that you could have acted without it, in cold blood. A chance circumstance could have had you meeting in the same holiday spot and from there grew the opportunity for vengeance.

A: You're wrong about the past, it doesn't stay the same. Time is a leprosy that disintegrates the past.

In cold blood I can tell you that you're off course, and your hypotheses are in urgent need of proof.

Q: Perhaps, but in my investigations diversions are useful. They make characters known; interesting details emerge simply in the choice of words. You corrected me before, using the terms of not socialising and denial. We can admit they're not expressions of hate, but they are of contempt.

I have to understand if you're capable of the crime I believe you committed. I could conclude that you're nowhere near capable. You want to show me that you're above it, you wouldn't have stooped to that level. But you could be below that level and so not have committed the crime. In that case, my accusation would be flattery, even a compliment to you.

Outside the scope of this investigation, you're

acquiring support and consideration from your past circles, people are following the case with approving comments.

A: Really? They're approving something I deny doing? I'm willing to start listening to you now. It's pleasant having someone interested in me. Being an unknown at the centre of attention, even for professional reasons, flatters the ego. It makes me feel important.

I'm incapable or I'm above it? I don't know how to respond. It seems to me, however, that you've been given a task beyond your capacities in having under investigation a person older and more experienced than you. I know about trials, and not from watching crime shows on television, but from belonging to the generation most put on trial in Italian history.

It'll seem strange to you, given my position of inferiority being under arrest, but I believe I have an advantage over you. I have a greater capacity for refuting accusations than you have of proving them.

You say that this accusation is gaining me some attention outside among the circles of past militancy. Why not also in the criminal world? The death of a traitor fits nicely into their code of behaviour.

And as for reputation, emerging from anonymity with your name in the papers? So much toilet paper, it lasts as long as the time you use it.

The celebrity that makes us unknowns memorable is being written up for life in the records of the police. That's where we can't be cancelled out, where we're in for perpetuity. I've been there for decades. I'm already a celebrity, there are many of us like that.

The Sicilian writer Leonardo Sciascia was a member of a parliamentary commission into the kidnapping of Senator Aldo Moro. He had a feeling of bleakness towards the guilty and their motivations. He couldn't, or didn't want to, elevate them to reasons. But he added his literary point of view that I've argued about with myself at length.

I'd better stop here. Are you interested in what I'm saying? I'm following my old starting point of reflection, a way of clarifying things with myself. It won't help your investigation.

Q: It interests me. Besides the objective of this conversation between interviewer and interviewee, I'm hearing a point of view about history.

A: Then I'll carry on. Sciascia maintains that a criminal political act, such as the kidnapping of Moro and the massacre of his police escort, concerns only those who committed it. Even if committed as a collective class action, the crime remains the responsibility of the individuals who committed it. It is and remains the responsibility of those individuals. From the human and literary point of view it's true. The shots fired in those actions continue to have repercussions in the hands of the participants.

But there are other contexts, to do with the offence of belonging to an armed gang. The State wanted to apply this as an aggravating factor to each and every member of the movement. I don't need to explain to you the consequences of this. As a member of an armed movement, I was condemned as responsible for whatever action it carried out, including those where I was not present.

In the trials of those years, life sentences were rained down on people who only had someone from the movement staying in their flat. Goodbye individual responsibility and so much for Sciascia, member of parliament for the Italian State. Whoever belongs to a law that condemns groups *en masse*, including those who haven't committed the specific crime, can't be an impartial judge of conscience.

The journalism of the day took the title of a German film to bundle together an entire decade between 1970 and 1980 as the "Years of Lead".

That journalism grouped into the spraying of lead a large part of the militant revolutionaries who were not members of armed cadres. Another headstone to place over the grave of individual responsibility.

To conclude, I consider myself responsible for what was committed in public in those years. But in assessing an era of collective action, it's also the positive results achieved by protesting on the streets, it's not only the crimes.

And what was Sciascia talking about? The emotional ricochet that armed action has on whoever carries it out. Political motivation doesn't protect the nerves of the participant from the consequences over time. They come to find that the actions once deemed necessary and urgent are today absurd. As time moves on it reveals what the political reason was cloaked in and isolates the participants. Those shots fired will continue to echo in the mind.

Sciascia is right on the human level: responsibility is individual. He was right on the literary level, too, as was established once and for all in *Crime and Punishment*.

He was wrong on the level of politics and the law. As a parliamentarian on a commission of inquiry he found himself on the wrong side for launching his conclusions. He was elected on the Radical Party ticket, he believed in the type of commitment of a writer. He was mistaken, because it denied his individuality, irreconcilable with belonging to a political party and an organ of the State. In his function of public investigator he wasn't a writer any longer. He could not expect to be neutral.

I am aware of having let myself get sidetracked into subjects that have kept me company for a long time. There's no chance to talk about them, so this has been an opportunity.

It's as if I were at the table of a restaurant bar one evening and was pouring my thoughts out in a monologue. I open my eyes and what do I find? A magistrate in front of me! What am I doing, collaborating with the authorities? Not in the way the words are used in judicial proceedings.

Putting aside the matter of personal considerations,

I'm revealing aspects of my character to you. But who cares about my character? Isn't it a waste of time listening to somebody ramble on who was caught up in the twentieth century?

Are you interested? I can offer you my character, but you won't be able to use it against me.

It's not about personality, I don't have one. Mine's multiple, like all of us from that turbulent era which was shaking the nobles from their saddles.

Q: So, you agree with Sciascia that every action falls back on whoever commits it. Whatever the motivation in the name of a public cause, it leaves the guilty person at the mercy of themselves. It's an important admission of your character. You declare yourself responsible for what you did personally, and also what your generation did. These assumptions of responsibility must have weighed on you for some time, to the point of making light of this case you're now involved in.

For you, being incriminated in a murder weighs almost nothing against the sum of what you've already wanted to assume. The struggle with total responsibility makes you invulnerable to the charge. Being restricted in solitary confinement has put no pressure on you whatsoever. You are paying for belonging to an era you defined as turbulent. You've clarified your character for me and also the personality expressed by your generation. I understand that your detention here brings no sense of shame.

A: Shame? Let me give you an instance. One Christmas Eve we went to our uncles' house to receive our presents. There were dozens of us at the time. One of the adults dressed up as Santa Claus and gave the presents out to us kids. Those of us who were already at school had to bring a letter with our New Year resolutions and we were asked to recite a poem. In those years you were taught to learn them off by heart. Every December we had to learn something for Christmas.

It was painful performing to the satisfied silence of the adults, but it was your contribution to the festivities.

Well, one time it was the turn of a boy to recite his poem and he didn't want to. His excuse was that they hadn't taught him one. They insisted he recite something, even just a few lines. So, in the usual satisfied silence the boy came out with the nursery rhyme about Easter, "*È Pasqua, è Pasqua!*" That's all he knew.

He was interrupted by a general sniggering that continued through his tears and sobs.

I can see that you also smiled.

I can't think of any worse shame than that of a child who's doing his best and finds the adults laughing in his face. Encouraged by them, the children also started to laugh. I'd like to know today if I too laughed then.

I can still remember the name and surname of the boy. He was younger than I was. His humiliation impressed itself on me, irredeemably.

Here at this table there's no shame. I'm doing my best and no-one's allowed themselves to laugh in my face.

Q: Did no-one try to comfort the child?

A: His mother. We had mothers then.

Q: We still have them.

A: Not like that child's or mine.

Q: A curiosity. You know poetry off by heart, yes?

A: A certain amount. I go over it in solitary there.

Q: Let's get back to the case. I think that you're still paying for belonging to that movement today.

A: Belonging to it, yes, I lived it out. It was so much a part of me that everything else was excluded. I'm from a city in the south, one of those that the force of it screaming turns the nervous system into an instrument with plucked strings. I'm also from a family that brought me up strictly, out of necessity.

These belongings of mine were suspended, I was no longer of a place, no longer had a personal history. I belonged to an era that was public.

I found my origins again afterwards; they'd become memories, empty vintage bottles.

As we talk, I forget I'm under a charge of murder. Earlier I imagined I was at the table of a restaurant bar delivering a monologue. Now it seems as if I'm in front of a silent audience, a crowd of absent people to whom I'm giving my testimony. Again, I realise there's a magistrate in front of me and I'm not worried whether he's listening with the others or not.

Perhaps you have shamanistic powers and can conjure up suspended states of consciousness. Or else it's me that feels invulnerable to the charge and can bypass dutiful replies.

I have no fear about the outcome of these days. The time in solitary doesn't weigh on me because it's still my time inside. I'm old enough not to be pawing the ground with impatience, wanting to prance around outside.

Q: If you've nothing to add, I consider this preliminary judicial investigation now over. I can tell you that I have no shamanic gifts, nor do I usually conduct such a wide-ranging interview with an accused. I don't consider your opening up to me a collaboration. You don't come anywhere near that.

You've given me a lesson of your point of view in political history, which isn't the same as that of a witness. A witness finds themselves by chance in a certain time and place. You, on the other hand, are a party in question to an era that was defeated and is forgotten. Your point of view is now clear to me, so I'm grateful for your digressions.

A: May I take advantage of your gratitude to ask you something? Could you leave me in solitary? I don't need to socialise with the other detainees or have more time for exercise.

I'd also like to offer you some advice. Have someone go with you to the Cengia del Bandiàrac. Go with the only man who can guarantee your safety. He's Diego Z, an alpine guide. I went with him my first time. Go and see how it is there and how it feels underfoot. Do it for yourself, not for the investigation.

Lastly, I would ask my solicitor not to put forward a request for bail. I prefer to leave here having been acquitted of any charge, and not because a lawyer has the ability to let me go home ahead of time.

Another letter, Sweetheart, to add to those I haven't sent. I'm still in solitary, so there's no way I can have any visits. Not that I want any, nor letters. This is a men-only place, a row of single cells like a monastery, but without the prayers. The monks here rely on solicitors, and they see to the prayers.

Mine is an experimental case. It's pushing a man to confess to a political crime, the last instalment of a forgotten era. They want to convince me that this is a way to conclude a history of judicial proceedings. The confession of a political vendetta would mark the end to a period that's remained open to this day. Not one of those who betrayed his comrades has met with any vengeance. It's still hanging in the balance.

And would a single act of vengeance balance things out? Would it outweigh the sentences served on the downside? No. But on the plus side, one act instead of none would be a specific symbol of greater weight. I'm surrounded by this line of reasoning, and, with my consent, they want me to give in to it.

And in a full confession there'd be the inner advantage of getting rid of a weight. But in his life this magistrate has certainly not come across a confession that led to a custodial sentence. Does he foresee some physical relief in discharging myself of a load off my insides, as if someone had constipation and a confession assisted a bowel movement?

He won't prevail over me with the shortcut of a confession.

If he doesn't acquit me, I'll go to court under the accusation. The novelty this time will be that I'm older than the judges. It's an advantage for me, I'd find them reduced in power and authority. When I was twenty, they had the power to take away a good part of my life out in the fresh air. Now all they can rake in are the crumbs.

Did you know that the accusation is that I pushed off a mountain path a comrade from long ago political struggles, one who then became an informer? At that time, we were friends. They used to say we were friends for life, but that expression wasn't enough for him, he wanted to give me life, a life sentence in prison. They also said we were blood brothers, but we never went through the ritual of cutting our palms and mixing our two bloods. He asked me, but I didn't want to. It would have excluded the other comrades.

In those turbulent years, friendship was an exchange of help knowing that it would be of immediate necessity with no time for explanations. We were united by a common will.

We were distanced at a stroke from our families, renouncing and turning our backs on a life of domesticity. We had a different way of belonging. Friendship substituted for family love, making the others a brother, father or a son.

We two were like that then. I'm writing this to explain things to you that have remained confused to me. I couldn't understand then how he could have torn himself away from us. Instead of sharing the defeat and punishment with us, he betrayed everyone, including me. He didn't forget anyone as he turned us in. And I understand it even less that I resent his turning us all in as a crime against me personally more than all the others. But I can tell you something about him.

He was a live wire, the opposite of me, and he knew how to attract the girls. He was inventive in chatting them up and, while I was there, he would say to ones he fancied, "You can take advantage of me, if you like." They would laugh and give in to him. Word got around, but when others tried it, it didn't have the same effect. Anyway, it became his nickname: "The advantage man."

You see, even after decades, I can't separate the friend from the traitor. I'm writing all this down for you in the hope that you'll be able to explain it to me.

I had been a monk for a long, long time. It was only interrupted when we got together and suddenly found ourselves without time zones between us. Then our times together were doubled, yours and mine, together at the same time.

More than being in the one place with you, what matters is being in the same minutes of the day. I love it to pieces asking you what time of day it is and to hear you say that it's the same as mine. I love to hear the annoyance in your voice when you tell me.

During the interview I started talking about Leonardo Sciascia, about the time when he stopped being a writer and became a parliamentarian. With you, however, I prefer to remember him as a writer. I was a very satisfied reader of his work. I like the brevity of his stories, their Sicilian flavour that doesn't descend into dialect. It's an inner Sicily. He talks about isolated heroes pitted against the way things are, and the way people get used to living with evil.

In words of his I only half remember, he writes that truth lies at the bottom of a well and, if you look in at the surface, you see the reflection of the sun or the moon. Then if you drop down into the well, you find neither one nor the other, but you find the truth. That's how it is, you have to drop down inside it or fall in. The magistrate, for example, questions me from behind the surrounding wall. He doesn't go inside; at most he leans over.

Sciascia wrote stories about detectives blessed with excellent powers of observation who discovered inextricable complexities. Society was a thorn bush, ready to prick the living and the dead.

The film versions of his novels miss the intensity of his descriptions, focusing instead on the corruption side.

With my magistrate it's more of a debate than an investigation. He still hasn't come up with any proof, so he creates a conversation about his hypothetical charge.

He proposes it and I dispose of it. But I have no hostility towards this man, who's the age of the son I don't have. I suggested he take a trip into the mountains. He's never been.

You learned from me, then decided that mountains weren't for you. But you did try them out and felt the satisfaction of putting your foot down correctly so that you didn't slip on the gravel.

I suggested the mountain to the magistrate not to put him in difficulty, but to have him realise a little better what he's accusing me of. He can even convince himself I'm guilty, but at least he'll know in what place the fall occurred.

The subject of tennis, which I enjoyed as a teenager, came up in our conversation. I never played it myself: then it was a sport for the few, you played it only in tennis clubs. Now it's everywhere, top players spring up from all social classes. It's become faster and more beautiful. I watch it on television, I don't go to the tournaments anymore. But we could go together sometime.

I ask myself why I like it. It's for the geometry of the trajectories that aim to find the most distant point in the court to the opposing player. The racquet is used like a club or as a caress. The sound of the strokes varies from a snap of the fingers to the swish of a handshake. The bounce of the ball makes the sound of a drop of water from a tap.

Here in solitary, I close my eyes and hear the sounds of a tennis match. They take me far away. This is a place where you can forget the meaning of the verb "to be able". Here you can do almost nothing.

If this incarceration lasts much longer, I'll resign myself to mailing you these letters, otherwise I'll be the postman and bring them myself. Kisses, Sweetheart.

Q: We are resuming the interview in the presence of the solicitor for the accused. I see you're letting your beard grow.

A: It helps me keep track of time.

Q: The lack of photographs from your youth is surprising. Apart from those group photographs of you all in the defendants' cages in the courtrooms, there are no private photos of you. While your written documentation is full of material – political analyses, publications, records of meetings. Between that era and the present that's the most striking difference.

During the search of your appartment there was not even one photograph album.

A: They're not taken in prison, except for identification.

Q: But for birthdays, Christmas, your parents?

A: I don't know what happened to them.

Q: There are no images of people on your cell phone. You take shots of places, dawns, sunsets, walls. Are you a lover of landscapes or do you still harbour clandestine habits?

A: I don't like photos of smiling faces grinning into the camera. These devices appear designed for private use, but they're open to anyone who wants to look into them. In addition, they constantly signal your location, so I use these contraptions warily.

Q: Devices, contraptions... even your language belongs to another era. Is it because you refuse to acknowledge modernity?

A: For me modernity means using these things with restraint, not with childish enthusiasm for the latest model.

Q: I get the impression you'd like to remove all trace of yourself. Perhaps even from the census, if that were possible. Is that it? A vocational desire to cancel oneself out?

A: Perhaps. The opposite is to emphasise one's presence, the obsessive desire to leave a trace, an image, an expression. The desire to add one's name to the list of celebrities, now so numerous as to be anonymous.

The current obsession to have oneself declared notable by others has nothing to do with me. I was part of a generation that acted in a collective name. So, I consider individualities and personalities not worth thinking about.

Q: From your tone of voice I'm trying to understand if you're saying this out of ideological reasons or a personal philosophical conviction. You know that you live in an era that's opposed to you?

A: Yes, and I believe I defend myself better than many people today blinded by spotlights and catwalks. I admire animals because they keep the show of originality to a minimum.

Q: Ah, yes, scratch away and in the end we're dealing with a return to nature.

Of all the recent defendants I've interviewed you're certainly the most eloquent by a long chalk.

A: Compliments from a public prosecutor to an accused make my skin crawl. Please spare me them.

Q: I meant to ask you this question last time we met and I forgot. Do you listen to music in the mountains?

A: No.

Q: And at home?

A: Not even there.

Q: It's strange to think of you as a young man without the company of music.

A: You can imagine it without dancing as well. I've never crossed the threshold of a discotheque.

Q: Were you all like that?

A: No, some of us liked concerts. They organised themselves to go and listen without paying. Music was a basic right for them.

Q: Yours was a very strange era.

A: I agree. It was strange to the point that a cell phone would not have been something you used in gaol to take smiling photos. I remember once I was freed along with others from a cage in a police van when a group of comrades attacked the squad cars guarding it. One broke the door off, shouting, "Abracadabra, everybody out!"

Q: Can we get back to music? As far as you know, was the man on the Cengia into it?

A: Yes, he was.

Q: What kind of music, do you remember?

A: He liked Pink Floyd, and some other groups I don't remember.

Q: And why not you?

A: If there's music on, I can't do anything else, not even wash my socks. I can't bear it in the background, it takes my attention away. So, I avoid it.

Q: The man on the Cengia continued having music with him. Just below the point where he fell we found a pair of earbuds and an MP3 player. Didn't you see it? It was just below you.

A: No. I wouldn't even recognise one.

Q: Who knows if he took it off before he fell or if it detached itself at the beginning of the fall. He could have taken it off in meeting you.

A: He didn't meet me.

Q: Do you have any idea what he was listening to?

A: No and I don't like guessing games.

Q: Pink Floyd, the music of your youth.

A: His youth.

Q: Yes, his. He was going towards the place he fell with the music he most loved in his ears. He was remembering your years together.

A: I see where you want to take this. You've found the soundtrack that links the past and the present. I was wondering where this digression was going. It wasn't a digression.

Q: This time, no. And where was I taking it?

A: To confirm there was a pre-arranged meeting on the Cengia? It didn't happen.

Q: This *is* a digression. How about the cinema? Was that also a distraction?

A: We used to go to the cinema. We shared the films out, the Russian ones in black and white; other contemporary ones on political themes.

Q: Such as?

A: I'm remembering at random. "*A Fistful of Dynamite*", "*Investigation of a Citizen above Suspicion*", "*Z*", "*The Working Class Goes to Heaven*", "*The Wild Bunch*".

Q: Pasolini?

A: Not so much, because he dealt with single characters from the subproletariat and during those years was overtaken by a new class consciousness.

Q: The man on the Cengia shared your tastes or did he stand out in that as well?

A: Yes and no, he liked the Japanese director Kurosawa. There were a lot of different cinemas then, cinema clubs and cheaper cinemas showing reruns in the outskirts. They were good places to set up regular meetings without the need to use the telephone. The funny thing about today is that communications are all intercepted, and yet people continue to talk so much and get themselves investigated for what they give away.

Q: And good for us.

We've ascertained that the victim was in the habit of hiking in the mountains and often went to the Val Badia in July. It's been ascertained that for some time you also were in the habit of going there. Had you never met there before?

A: No, and if it was true, I wouldn't have recognised him. People's features change over the years. Besides, when I'm hiking up there I look at the ground and where I'm putting my feet. If I cross paths with someone, I greet them without looking up. I recommend it to everyone who goes hiking in mountains; keep your eyes on the ground and, if you want to look around and raise your eyes, then stop.

Q: You could have met him in the valley below, say in San Cassiano, La Villa, Corvara. And decided to follow him.

A: Unlike him, my features have changed little over the years, I'm still thin and my hair hasn't fallen out. I don't have a beard or wear glasses. He could have recognised me without my knowing it.

Q: So, you're saying the opposite could have happened? The victim recognised you and instead of changing his holiday spot, he stayed in the same place at the same period?

A: You're calling a victim someone who set off alone into that tight spot. A victim is someone who's run over on a pedestrian crossing.

Q: I see you're paying close attention to my choice of words.

A: Because I like this language of ours, its precision protects us from falsehoods. Language is a system of exchange, similar to money. The law punishes those who print counterfeit notes but allows those who deal in language falsely to circulate freely. I protect the language I use.

Q: Therefore, if you don't use language falsely, you also never lie?

A: What have lies got to do with it? I'm talking about the definition of a word. The word victim, for example. If you use the word inappropriately, then you're not telling a lie, you're mistaking the meaning of the word.

Q: Alright, let's get back to the point. Perhaps that man had known you for some time and he was following your tracks.

A: Are you switching the roles here? You should read the charge sheet again. To keep within your new reconstruction, we need to know what passes through the head of a man who carries the weight of shame around, who turned the lives of others upside down for decades while his own was untouched.

Q: Those lives were already upside down.

A: Do you think he was trying to approach me? Make himself known? I can tell you of an episode – you don't have to believe me. A year ago, I went to the launch of a book on the history of those years. At the end of it, a man of about my age came up and said he'd been in the same movement as me in the same city and recognised me because I'd changed so little. I asked him which territorial section he was involved in, and he said that he was an undercover policeman.

It didn't surprise me, we budgeted for it, the doors of our section were always open. It was enough for a new recruit to be introduced by someone who was already a member. The movement was growing like this and didn't issue membership cards. What mattered to us was the contribution someone could make, their commitment and dedication. Whoever came along out of curiosity or simply to say they belonged soon left.

We were open to all, but the decisions were taken by a narrow group of proven trustworthiness.

That man didn't want to apologise, he wanted to greet me fair and square after so many years. He wasn't there on duty, he had already retired.

I'm telling you all this in order to say how I reacted. I didn't. I didn't ask his name when he started or when he stopped. I put my hand on his shoulder and said goodbye.

I appreciated his sincerity, a salaried employee of the Ministry of the Interior who had taken on a task with the risk of exposure. The meeting ended there.

It has nothing to do with the present case. That man was on the side of the State, not ours. We had our own moles in their apparatuses. Nothing at all like one of us who turned traitor.

Q: If he had been discovered, how would you have reacted?

A: We're not at that level of confidence. That man was carrying out his role as a spy. We would have questioned him to see what information he'd given out.

Q: And then?

A: Let's change the subject. I told you about how I reacted in that instance because I found myself in it. I don't know how I'd behave when meeting one of our movement who had reneged to the point of betrayal. I can't know beforehand. I can't predict my reactions. Even now with you I improvise.

If I'd thought beforehand about how I'd react to being interviewed on a charge of murder, I'd have seen myself closing up, refusing to talk. However, here I am, telling things to a magistrate he wouldn't have known. So I can't say how I would react.

These interviews have become an opportunity for me to talk about myself. I'd also say this, I have a close relationship with a woman who lives some distance away. We talk about everything except the past. And while I take in the questions here, I seem to be explaining my times to her as well, although she has never asked about them.

Beyond here and the obligation to sit opposite you, I rule out the possibility of sharing something of that past with someone I don't know.

Q: Let's move on with the hypothesis, shall we? Say that man decided to hang around, certain that he's not been recognised. He could have followed you into the mountains from a distance. He still doesn't know what he wants to do with this discovery. Perhaps he thinks of a chance meeting.

A: You continue to play around with this hypothesis. When will you get to the thesis?

Q: Hypotheses let one explore, but theses wait for what they can discover. So that man follows you. He even goes to the bar of the *pensione* you're staying in. Perhaps he even hears you say to the person serving that you're going to the Cengia the following day.

A: Before I was the ill-intentioned one, now it's him. Where are you going with this?

Q: I'll tell you. That man on the Cengia del Bandiàrac went ahead of you on purpose, knowing that you'd be going there. And at that point he turned around and there you met. You were face to face with him and didn't know what was happening until he told you his name. He was there to test your reaction at a point where it was impossible to avoid each other. He had hunted you. What would the reaction be? Anything was possible, from a fight to a reconciliation. You reacted knowing that you were playing with the life of one or both of you. So, what did happen? Would you like to tell me?

A: Having established on my part that this meeting didn't happen, I still don't know what my reaction would have been.

Q: I'm going to insist that it did happen. You didn't follow him, but he went ahead of you. You told me that in your first interview, which I went and listened to again. You were already telling me how things had gone. That man was in front of you.

How did it go, face to face on the Cengia? You understood that from there only one of you would return and locked together in a hand-to-hand fight would have seen both of you fall. So, what to do? Tell me.

A: Why don't you tell me, seeing as you already know.

Q: You bent down to pick up a rock. But you didn't pick up a rock, did you?

A: No? What did I pick up?

Q: You were more practical and quicker. You grabbed a handful of dust and threw that in his face. He was blinded.

While he wiped his eyes you had time to push him off the precipice.

A: You have talent as a storyteller. You should follow the career of some of your colleagues that have started writing crime fiction with positive results for the bank account. You could call this one *Duel on the Cengia*.

Q: The post-mortem revealed traces of dust in the eyes. A person who falls shuts their eyes to protect them, they don't keep them open. I went up on the Cengia with your friend the alpine guide, a difficult experience for me. I had to combat my fear. Your friend is very capable. He kept me securely linked to him, step by step. I came to the spot where the man fell and collected some of the dust. It coincides with what we found.

A: Now you've gone too far. You've discovered that the mountain has the same dust on the Cengia as it does below the precipice. That body would have been covered in dust, soil and gravel all over it. You talk about the eyes. And in the ears, the nose, the mouth you found nothing? You're fixated on your hypothesis, but if you take this idea of dust in the eyes as proof, then you better bring a handful to court to throw in the judge's eyes as well.

Q: It's difficult to arrive at some point with you where we can meet. I'm saying this was a case of self-defence. You happened to be the one who was quicker to put it into practice. I'm offering you the means of acquittal.

A: As well as having to admit to murder. The papers will write it up like a film script. But you need my consent to make this into your masterpiece. Take me back to the cell.

Q: The papers are already onto it. I can show you the whole page of one newspaper: your photo, mine, the mountain. In solitary you haven't been keeping up. If my reputation upsets you, it's already launched. There's no need to add your admission of guilt. The case has already excited the public interest. However it goes, they're waiting for you out there. Your anonymity is over, if not lost altogether.

A: It's quite secure, thank you. You only have to avoid collaborating in the publicity over the accident. The papers will quickly forget and move on to the next crisis.

Q: That's true. But if we go to court the press will treat the public hearing as a circus of your word against mine. Your position will give greater visibility to me and annoyance to you by transforming the case into a duel between prosecution and defence.

A: Now hold on with the duels. They take place between people armed with the same weapons, and on the same ground. Between prosecution and defence, it isn't a duel, nor a duet. I'm struggling for my good name and my liberty. You are not.

Q: So be it, no duel then, but an admission on your part would lessen the case and the attention it gets. Your obstinacy will only make it more clamorous. This time I'm sending you back to the cell with the recommendation for further reflection. You can come out of this intact and more quickly if you agree to the thesis of self-defence. I'll be your counsel for the defence and argue that in the circumstances you had no choice.

A: But you'll have to demonstrate one way or another that this man was so twisted as to think up this kind of encounter.

Q: I'm at a good point. I showed the man's photo to the server in the *pensione* bar, Signora Lavinia. She can't rule out not having served him. Given the growing publicity, it will be simple to persuade her to strain the memory and remember him fully. You'll know that memories are reconstructions. An investigator has to help out in this regard.

That man came to the bar in your *pensione*. Once this is established, we can definitively discount the chance meeting on the Cengia.

A: You can discount it for leaning heavily on a witness. A huge number of customers pass through that bar, it's convenient, it's by the car park. And why should this man throw himself into a business that puts his life at risk?

Q: That's where his personality comes in. He's been in the witness protection programme for years with another identity and place to live. For decades he's looked over his shoulders for people like you. It so happens that he bumps into one of the people he informed on without being recognised. He turns the positions round: he can follow your tracks and in a certain sense he can go hunting you. He's nothing more to fear. He can even think of a place to meet you face to face. It's a liberation for him. He can come out into the open after years in hiding.

He showed he was a singular character even when he belonged to your hardline movement. The only coincidence I'm prepared to consider is that the two of you have the same attraction to mountains and the same habit of going there alone.

As to wanting to meet one of the comrades from the movement again, it isn't an isolated case. As a magistrate I know of similar cases, informers who encounter old comrades and face up to them. By now they're weaker, exhausted after long years in prison. Their reaction is a passive one. Surprised in the moment, they don't react. But you had the time to overcome any feeling of surprise and think up the idea of a chance meeting in some isolated spot.

Or else it happened in a different way. In a casual meeting in the valley he believed he'd been recognised by you, but that you'd pretended you hadn't. So he discounted the chance encounter and decided he was being stalked by you. In reconstructing the movements here, it transpires that there was a change of address about a year ago after taking a holiday in the mountains.

A: Who, me?

Q: No, him. He moved house in a hurry about a year ago, his friends say. And imagine this: he shaved off his hair and grew a beard.

Did he suspect he'd been recognised a year ago in Val Badia?

A: He went back on his tracks? To my stalking him?

Q: You recognised that man a year ago.

A: I wouldn't even recognise my own shadow.

Q: You did recognise him and pretended not to. He knew you had and went on the run, changing his address and his looks. And, thus transformed, he came back this year and started to stalk you. You spoke in the bar of your planning to go up on the Cengia. Did you do it on purpose so he would hear? You recognised him even with his changed appearance.

A: Not at all. In the bar I drink my beer at a table, not at the bar itself. I exchange a couple of words with Lavinia.

I don't say where I'm going. I can pass for an expert, so try to avoid any guest in the *pensione* asking to come with me.

Q: I'm missing which of the two of you had the motive. By the way, the man was armed with a knife. It was found directly below the Cengia. Did he threaten you with it? Do you carry a knife in the mountains?

A: No. I've already told you what I carry in my rucksack.

Q: Now, you met on the mountain. I have to understand how much intention there was and on the part of whom between the two of you. I believe that exposing yourselves to danger in that isolated country authorises you alpinists to a different set of rules. Two people who met in the city would take each other to court, but in the mountains they would kill each other. But this isn't the Wild West, even mountains are subject to the same jurisdiction.

A: You're right, it is a land apart. The inhabitants of alpine villages look to settle their differences in the old manner, without bringing in the law and the police. They don't take the power of the State that represents them too seriously.

Q: I must take it seriously. The State is the motive for which the citizen delegates the use of force. It's the job of the State to make sure that the laws are respected and to put right any wrongs. Whoever transgresses and takes the law into his own hands in the mountains is committing a crime.

The State has an agreement with everyone. Even the revolutionaries who want to take power keep the State. No-one has the right to create their own idea of justice. You are here because I suspect you of committing such a violation. The mountains are not a place of diminished legislation.

A: You don't know the place. You don't even know the area encompassed by your investigation. From my point of view, you know nothing. But you have the power of decision even without knowing.

This is the perfect finishing line for power, coming to the maximum level of incompetence and deciding on everything. I see society as a construction where the more it proceeds upwards the poorer become the materials.

You behave as if you know how things are. But it's a fiction of yours and the office you fill.

Q: You may convince yourself of this fiction. But for me, on the other hand, it's the function the State assigns me.

A: You place it on an altar and make an idol out of it. It pays you a salary and will give you a decent pension. I remain a layman with regard to the State, I don't share your liturgy of it.

Q: You think I've made an idol of the State? I'd define myself as an idealist. I believe in the State and its institutions. I'm a functionary, not a priest in a cult. But it's funny how you invert the roles here: you, the idealist of a failed revolution, now claim to be the cynical realist.

A: Good philosophical chat, right for the drawing room. But we aren't in a drawing room. I arrived here this morning with my wrists handcuffed and I'll leave like that. You can forget these details, I can't.

Q: Sometimes this investigation turns into a kind of debate, but my intention remains that of establishing the facts and the verification of whether a crime has been committed or not.

I don't forget your condition as a detainee. The solicitor behind you here to represent you and the record of the questions and replies are here to witness what we're doing. And here we must finish.

You have much to consider. It would behove you to give me the answer of self-defence, one of the two I outlined. Both are good for me. It doesn't matter how things really went as long as we arrive at a truth for the court.

If you maintain your denial, I will decide which of the two pleas; either he chose the confrontation, or you did. The next interview will be the last, then I'll close the investigation and pass the documentation on for judicial proceedings.

Sweetheart, I have to have one more chitchat with the examining magistrate and then it's all over, one way or another. It seems this business has interested the press. He's insisting on my admitting to self-defence and then I'll be acquitted. Your views matter to me and I'd like to know what you think I should do. Once released, will you give me a hug or say how disappointed you are?

I can't ask you, so I have to get there by thinking of you. I can get out after confessing to having bumped into the man and caused him to fall. Or else I don't get out, continue to deny any meeting and go to trial, and possibly even be found guilty.

How would you proceed? I'm mulling it over. I don't know how you'd take to me confessing. I believe, however, I know how you'd take my refusing to come to a deal over the accusation. Yes, I think I know. You'd be in agreement with me.

So my decision is to continue as I have up till now.

Thank you for having helped me make the choice. If I have to go to court, I'd prefer you not to come even then and see me in the dock, with the press around the last Mohican out of the reservation to avenge himself on the Paleface.

But it's pointless creating pipe dreams. One thing at a time.

Today the magistrate was after photographs. He didn't find any at home, nor on my phone. There aren't any from the past and the few of my parents were sequestered at the time of the searches and mass arrests. So they've gone missing.

I did print out those of us together for you and deleted them from the phone. They're now hidden away. No-one is going to take away those of us together.

I told the magistrate that I don't like pictures of faces grinning at nothing. It's not true. Your face smiles at me even when you're serious. It lights up for me even when it's in the dark.

I've safeguarded you from questions and searches.

In early-twentieth-century photographs, faces don't smile. They stand there stiffly, even anxious about being portrayed. When did smiles start to appear in photographs? When did people become relaxed? Was it with the advent of the cinema and its posters and imitating the actors? Odd questions, but I'm passing them on, perhaps you'll have an answer.

And a provisional balance sheet of my time here? Two lost buttons and one tooth. They were loose before.

I've also lost a little weight. The diet in here is restricted, so as not to feed your hopes.

When they take me to the magistrate I'm forced to hold my trousers up. I have to shuffle my feet because they take away your laces. Belts and laces are prohibited.

These little inconveniences can be humiliating, but not with me. It's they who should be embarrassed putting a man in this position. I don't think it happens with them, so nor with me. The humiliation score is nil–nil. In the meantime, they serve to remind me I have a body.

In the other prison before, the magistrates came to us to do their questioning. It was too complicated to organise enough escorts for the transfer of such dangerous prisoners as we politicos were considered. Now they take me to the magistrate's office and bring me back again. They put my wrists in a pair of metal handcuffs that come from the past. They should be in a museum. Out of curiosity, before I had them on my wrists, I did an online search once and found a pair on offer for seventy euros.

The escort puts the cuffs on in the cell and then attaches a chain to take me out, following behind. I found them heavy as a young man, now not so much. I must have grown used to them. Now they're just awkward, as if they were putting white gloves on me.

They're there to stop people escaping, explains the young escort officer who wants to show some consideration to an old man. That's fine, I tell him, I come from a long line of fugitives. I made it up that my father escaped from a Fascist prison and my grandfather from a Bourbon one. The times don't add up historically, but who studies history today? It's evaporated.

So, properly in irons, I'm taken across the city in a police van. I can't see out, there are no windows in the inside cage. But I can hear the outside, cars, sounds, voices. I feel like a deep-sea diver in his diving suit crossing an aquarium.

There was some traffic today, it was raining and drivers were agitatedly sounding their horns. Their impatience made me smile. I'm in time and in the pure temple of patience. On the prison gates there should be written a variation of the words Dante reads over the entrance to hell: Abandon all impatience, ye that enter.

And so it happens, because in prison time happens. You're inside a cell, a guest of time.

These trips in irons through the middle of a city and its impatient people are a diversion for me and I find myself smiling. The young officer escorting me looks over and shakes his head. He must think I have a screw loose.

By the way, I must thank you for that book you sent me this spring, Sidney Lumet's *Making Movies*. It's made me a better viewer. Now I see screens where there are none. The room around me is like a piano accordion. It expands for hours in the plaster walls and I can see a spread of landscapes. I can focus on a centimetre and it becomes a valley. Then at other times it's closed tight as a fist. You turn off the light, the darkness cancels everything around you, then other things come from far off.

In this moment, with a decision made together, the room is large and I'm taking huge breaths.

Q: The interview is resumed. The solicitor for the accused is present. I confirm this is the last occasion we will meet, then my investigation is over.

Today you come out of solitary. Either you will be transferred to the normal detention cells with the other detainees, or you will be released on bail. Your choice of judicial position will decide which of the two it will be.

In these days I've gone back to hiking in the mountains among the Dolomites here which, up till now, I'd only seen from the bottom of the valley. I've discovered that I like it and can understand you alpinists a little. Climbing up I can concentrate better and gather my thoughts together.

I've been thinking about you. I can say that I've had you as company. I went alone to the summit of the Lavarella peak following the route on the map.

I suffer from vertigo, I think. When I lean out from a

balcony the feeling of empty space disturbs me. Going up step by step, however, looking carefully at the ground as you advised me, breathing in a regular rhythm, I felt no vertigo at all.

I've discovered that the descent is more demanding because that empty space is in front of you while you're walking down. So I've learned something useful for myself as well as the investigation.

Besides, it's the same for me in all my cases. Crimes are repeated, the articles in the Penal Code are the same, but not the people. Each different human being is a unique variant and each one requires a new side of me. They put me to the test and I have to say that, like you, I also improvise.

I think that experience rightly consists in the ability to surprise oneself, creating an approach you hadn't seen before. Experience doesn't have a catalogue of ready moves; on the contrary, you must have faith in the ability to improvise.

So, I come to my question. Do you miss the mountains you recommended to me?

A: I've climbed them, several more than once. Others have defeated me. I'm not biting my nails to start hiking again.

Unlike for you, they've always been there for me. If you were the detainee, you'd miss them out of wanting to go there again, after that first time. I was like that at first, I couldn't get enough of them.

Nowadays I don't miss those I can still get to. At my age prison takes little away from life. A suitable punishment would be to take away the mountains of my past, wipe them off my hands and my breath. However, they're stored up there in the hold of my senses. Your power over me is limited to the small space of the present.

Q: From your reply, I take it that age gives you an unfair advantage over the young.

A: In the case of prison, yes. But have no fears about reaching my advantage. Enjoy the disadvantage of your youth. But why would it be unfair?

Q: It doesn't depend on merit, but on fate, including one's health.

A: Then life is unfair.

Q: Don't you think it is? It multiplies inequalities rather than reduces them and then mixes them up at random. Why do you deserve to be older?

A: I don't follow you. I'm a single case, there are worse ones. I believe I'm in the middle of cases born earlier, therefore nominated to die sooner. In this moment I recognise my advantage over you. Soon I'll disappear and my advantage with it and it'll be your turn to profit from lasting longer. I'm at the end of my turn and I don't envy those coming to take my place.

Q: Alright, we'll leave it at that. You feel yourself more capable in these discussions. Go ahead, I don't feel the need to be superior.
So where are we up to? Have you made your decision?

A: No, there wasn't one to make. I had nothing to do with this accident. I was there by chance, and I behaved in line with my civic duty.

Q: Is this your final word?

A: It was my first word and I've been repeating it now for a long time.

Solicitor: Excuse me, I have to leave for a few minutes.

Q: Alright, please go ahead. We'll pause the interview. What were you best in at school?

A: I went to school on foot for a good couple of kilometres. The material I was best in was my footwear.

Q: You were good at maths.

A: Have you looked at my reports?

Q: Part of the research. You didn't always walk. You also went by scooter.

A: Never had one.

Q: No, you didn't, but your friend did and he gave you a lift.

A: Congratulations, you've traced a means of transport of fifty years ago.

Q: Your friend wasn't very good at maths. You helped him, didn't you?

A: You've discovered our bargain. I did his exercises in exchange for a place on the saddle.

Q: I'm not moved by your tone. Bargain has nothing to do with it. You were friends for life.

A: Life is a fragile thing.

Q: There's a sign in maths that's also a symbol. It's two dashes or hyphens, one on top of the other, and it means equality. As boys you used that symbol between you. In that man's house I found exercise books from secondary school bound up by a ribbon. There were also letters and a diary. At that time, when people still wrote letters, you signed off not with your names but an equals sign, meaning parity, a draw.

A: An equals sign doesn't mean equality or a draw. It means an equivalence in personal values, and it's on those you establish a relationship governed by the sign of those two little dashes. Equality is a political idea. If two numbers are equal in maths, then they're not two.

Q: There were two different hands in those exercise books. I imagine one of them was yours.

A: You don't imagine, you already know.

Q: Your relationship was very close. In one page of the diary there's a description of your climbing the Gran Sasso in summer taking the route called "Direttissima". You came down the same way. He writes that he was slower going up but faster than you on the descent. Would this be an example of equivalence?

A: It is, but I don't remember it. I've been up and down that route many times in recent years.

Q: He writes that you weren't roped together, but you went ahead because you already knew the "Direttissima" route.

A: It's possible, but if I knew the route before he did, there's no equivalence anymore.

Q: He writes that it became windy and you were cold.

A: It happens. In those days you dressed in what you had. The aim was speed.

Q: He offered you his windjammer, which you refused.

A: It's obvious I didn't need it. Through you, however, I come to know of the existence of a diary.

Q: Don't you recall those first trips in the mountains?

A: I'm not happy about the existence of that diary, nor that you've read it. So I'm going to make no effort to remember. The mountains aren't a butterfly collection, one climb cancelling out another.

When you've finished digging about in the archaeological remains of half a century ago, would you tell me what use you want to make of it and which section of the museum it should go in?

Q: This isn't archaeology. It's the reconstruction of a very close and intense friendship at the age when solid emotions develop.

A: I'm waiting to hear from you shortly that we were intimately involved.

Q: It wouldn't add anything to the picture of an exclusive understanding between the two of you. But it explains to me the maelstrom of emotions that was set off when you met again that first time. Because there was a first time due to pure coincidence. Then there was the last on the Cengia.

A: And the question?

Q: There isn't one. This is my conclusion and I'm asking you to admit it's true.
  I've gone into your past and I can say that I've felt like an intruder. I reached my conclusion with the feeling of

having violated something intimate – a strange sensation for an investigator.

I've rummaged about in the lives of two people who have shared an intensity that I couldn't even imagine. This relationship of yours has given me an insight into understanding the emotional charge of your generation. And you allowed me to. I can say that you even guided me into that inextricable knot of driving forces, public and private.

Now I'm asking you to round off my conclusion. You can take your hands away from your face and from what is blocking the truth.

A: Take me back to the cell, please.

Q: Wasn't a draw reached on the Cengia?

A: An equivalence was destroyed, yes. Now please take me back to the cell.

Solicitor: I'm back in my place.

Q: I'm telling you now this has been my last effort. I've failed and you have won. I don't have enough evidence to take this to trial. For me your guilt is certain, but it's impossible to link that to a guilty verdict in court.

I can confirm that it's also impossible to prove the hypothesis that you met on the Cengia by chance. But it's also impossible to prove the encounter was premeditated.

And I have to confess that I twisted your arm in taking advantage of your refusing a professional counsel to defend you. Such a lawyer would have stopped me earlier. I was also cheating. It wasn't possible to perform a forensic examination on the man's face. The head was never found. The body had disintegrated over a fall of hundreds of metres. Rain did the rest. The alpine rescue squad recovered only pieces. It was as if he had exploded.

If it was a crime, then you've succeeded. I give up. My capabilities aren't up to it.

Procedural truths are often sketchy, they depend solely on what comes to be written down in the record. So judicial errors can creep in. But here the truth of the records at my disposal is directly opposed to the reality. For me you are guilty of murder, but I have to release you.

You'll shortly return to prison only to go to reception for the formality of release.

In the meantime, I'll ask you a question that may

seem strange. Do you know Pascal, the French mathematician who dedicated himself clinically to relations with the divinity?

A: I've read bits of his *Pensées*. But if you asked me questions as teacher to pupil, then I'd fail.

Q: He makes a very appealing argument. That is, to act and think as if God exists. He adopted this style of belief. He prayed, loved and behaved as if God existed. With his "as if", Pascal raised the fiction into a rule for life. His wasn't a hypothesis, because they have to be examined and verified. It's a fiction, chosen deliberately to resolve a relationship with what isn't given one to know.

When questioning, on the other hand, a magistrate acts on the basis of a hypothesis about the responsibility of the accused. He verifies it and decides whether to go for trial or release.

Thinking of you I was reminded of Pascal and his choice of acting "as if". I find I have to forego the certainty of knowing, so I'm out of the field of hypotheses. But I act and think as if you were guilty. It's my fiction. It's a fiction you also practise, only you act as if you weren't guilty. We've arrived at a point together: two sceptics who act like Pascal in the face of truth. In my case, as if you did; in yours, as if you didn't.

A: Sceptics, you say? But we haven't been in a classroom debating across the same table. You can go home, I can't; you can talk to other people, I can't. You want me to admit to murder, I don't. You are the State, I am not. The only "as if" that I can imagine is that on leaving here we act as if we'd never met.

Q: No need to get angry. You've won.

A: I haven't won. There was nothing to win. What I had to do was lay myself open to proof. There's an oriental proverb that says if the waters rise, the boat had better do the same.

There's no such word as win or conquer in the mountains. There's only a draw between your efforts and the difficulties of the climb.

These weeks in a cell for twenty-three hours a day haven't been a waste of time. I've used them to the very best of my abilities.

The word win can apply to you, not to me.

Q: How does it feel to be a free man?

A: I've been free all the time. My freedom isn't within the constraints you impose by insisting on custody. What I will appreciate with relish is the first beer in the nearest bar to the exit.

Q: One day, outside the roles we now have, will you tell me the truth of how it really went?

A: Even beyond the roles we now occupy, you're still a magistrate.

I know of a magistrate who met a group of his old revolutionary comrades for dinner. He'd served with them as a militant when a young man. They got to telling old stories.

The day after, that magistrate had several participants at that dinner arrested. They'd talked too much. It wasn't as if he were undercover. Those comrades knew he'd become a magistrate. But they believed in a bond of loyalty to the past. In that they were mistaken. That magistrate had formed an understanding with the establishment that undid any previous ties.

There's no occasion between you and me when we'll ever come back to this business.

Q: Not even in the mountains? If it happened we went together, seeing as you recommended me to go up there.

A: You should hope not to meet me in the mountains given the charge you've tried to prove against me.

Q: Then I have this to say to you. This discussion has been my penultimate attempt.

I told you you were acquitted so you would lower your guard and allow me under your defences. But you've resisted my Trojan horse.

I'm not releasing you but sending you for trial on the charge of premeditated murder. You will return to prison in the normal cells.

A: So, the beer's postponed then?

Sweetheart, I just telephoned you, but wasn't able to say anything other than I've been released.

Journalists were waiting for me outside the prison, but I managed to avoid them by going out of another gate accompanied by – you'll never guess who – the magistrate who's been questioning me.

He's tried everything during these weeks. The last was a real piece of theatre. He started by saying that he was releasing me and that I'd won. There was insufficient evidence against me to bring it to trial. Then he asked me if, meeting outside the walls in the open, as equal citizens, I'd be able to tell him how it really was. I told him no. Then he turned the tables on me. It wasn't true he was releasing me; he was going to send me for trial instead.

He admitted he tried the expedient of saying he was releasing me to get me to relax and give way on some points.

I was upset for him. A man in the judiciary tries to

inveigle a man under lock and key? I was a pawn in his game who couldn't be moved. So he has me believe the game is up.

Then how come I'm out? Because it was true about my release. I wasn't sent back to the cell; they took me to reception and returned what they'd confiscated at the time I was admitted.

And at reception I found the magistrate. He told me that there were journalists at the main gate and he'd take me out in his service vehicle by another gate. I didn't ask him if this was another of his clever manoeuvres. This exit could also have been a ruse. However, it was real, there were journalists at the main gate, so they'd been told of my release.

He asked me if he could take me anywhere. I said I was going back to the mountains. So we set off, then he asked if we could have dinner together. I said yes, if we paid our own bills.

He asked me about the mountains. Then more questions, but of a different nature, using the verb with the Latin root for asking to know, not obtain.

Encounters are like books. And rivers. You never put your foot in the same one twice, a Greek philosopher said. And you never climb the same mountain twice. It's different, like reading Pinocchio at age ten and reading it at age fifty.

For the mountains he'll climb, I told him not to use the word "do". He shouldn't say "I've done that one". It was the world that thought of doing it.

We stopped at a trattoria. He asked me about Communism. To him it seems an idea against nature, because possession is human instinct. A child learns straightaway to say that something is "mine". They say it with conviction and an emphasis on the "m". How can Communism repress this natural impulse? He thought his reasoning was insuperable.

On the television they were showing a quiz programme with prizes.

Communism? It's not a question, but an answer. I told him my point of view, in between the beer trickling down my throat like a blessing. I let out a burp and he laughed, saying this was a good start to a reply.

So I told him my version. A child has many natural instincts. They'll say "It's mine" even about a toy that doesn't belong to them. They try it on, testing the limits, the limits of what's permissible.

Then they suddenly slip from your hand and run away, following the instinct for freedom, but you catch them before they're run over by a car.

They also have an instinct to wet the bed, so we instruct them not to. We're a species that tries to educate these instincts. Communism is an education in equalising basic conditions and starting points.

It's not a necessary thing that the means of production of goods and services be in private hands and those who invoice things as "mine". They can also be in public hands.

People shipwrecked on an island practise dividing up necessities into equal shares. It's a recognition that stops people killing one another.

It was like talking to a child. He listened closely to me and was amazed.

In the meantime, we'd ordered, he was having *pappardelle al sugo* and I was having *spaghetti aglio e olio*, with added hot peppers.

The dishes arrived. He added black pepper to his and I sprinkled some chopped hot peppers on my spaghetti. Then, as usual, I brushed my eyes with my fingers, with the usual stinging result.

I told him about the feeling of brotherhood. It's one of the words of the French Revolution – liberty, equality, fraternity – but it's different from the first two. You can fight to obtain liberty and equality or defend them. But not with fraternity.

Then what is it? It's the sentiment that holds the fibres of a community together, it reinforces the unity and produces the energy to fight for liberty and equality. Fraternity is the political sentiment *par excellence*. It doesn't exclude anyone. A Kurdish poster says that their victory doesn't depend on the number of enemies killed, but the number of enemies who unite with them. Even an enemy can be included in the brotherhood.

No programme can construct it, though, if it doesn't come by itself.

Communism is a fraternity, a brotherhood. When it loses that, it immediately stops and reverses into hierarchies and new privileged classes.

The beer and the peppers in the spaghetti had warmed my breath up, I was talking in a low voice under the noise of the place. He was straining to hear me and was leaning forwards. Perhaps he had a recorder. But he didn't ask me to speak any louder.

There was a personal curiosity in him that pushed me to have him hear my point of view, but he was still a magistrate. What happened to some comrades at dinner who were talking about an incident in the past in the company of one of them who had become a magistrate wasn't going to happen to me. The day after he had them arrested.

For me the past is fine as it is – dead and buried like a nail in wood.

My magistrate thought for a bit, then he said, "You speak about liberty, equality and fraternity. For me the key word is justice. I see the history of society under that aspect. We fight for a justice that's divided into equal parts and this is what produces liberty. It's always the same old story, don't you think?"

I don't know if you'd agree with him or me, but this is what I said: "You're of the right age, middle age, to talk about the same old story. For me things are like this: it's always the same story, but a new one. I know this as a reader. I read variations of stories already told, about love, travel, exile, punishment, discovery. But they're variations on the theme, therefore new.

"Life has the same effect on me. It repeats the same

lessons and I marvel at its capacity to respond to the details in the frame fixed to the wall. Old age in a solitary-confinement cell is suited to perceiving the nuances in hours that can't be repeated. I know that one day I'll remember this time under arrest with affection."

The trattoria started to empty and we each paid our own bill. They also had rooms for the night and I booked one. Before we separated, he asked me if he could shake my hand. I told him I was sorry, but for me it was a no.

"I understand," he said. "Up to the last you didn't want to help me arrive at the truth. It's your right, given the cost that would come with it. It's only out of curiosity that I ask: were you close to telling me?"

I told him no.

"So there was a truth," he added. And then, standing on the threshold of the place he asked me if there were any inferences I'd left that he'd missed. I told him that we continually leave traces, because we're a species that wants to leave them.

"Like tonight?" he asked. I spread my arms out in a gesture and turned my back on him. Good night.

You told me you liked tennis, while my game is football. But the role I prefer is referee. From when I was a boy I was fascinated by his renunciation of playing, his running about for nothing in the middle of the teams. He was there so that the match would be fair.

The only strange thing was the whistle. It sounded like a policeman on point duty. Another sound would be better, even a bell. I watched the ref instead of following the game. He wasn't above the opposing sides, he was right in the middle of them, without any global vision. He was whistled at and ran risks. He couldn't smile or celebrate.

I still think today that the aim and function of the State is that of referee, to allow the participants to live life out according to the rules. It's naïve of me, I can clearly see inequality, but I continue to cheer for the referee.

For more than half my life I've studied law in order to deal out justice in a form nearest to the letter. If you look to balance the weights in the scales of justice, the Penal Code isn't dry as dust. I consider my work a civic duty. I profess a devotion to justice that others express in their faith.

In these weeks I've come up against another desire for justice that claims to dictate the law. Your system of justice has failed, but it's not for that I write it off as utopian. When the criteria of justice overwhelm people's lives, having them serve decades in prison, then one can't speak of utopia. For your generation, you tried to live a different reality. You were all convinced you possessed a different justice. And you pursued it without any gain.

Today the prisons are only full because of crimes committed for personal gain to the disadvantage of others. The sentences your movement served for quite different motives show a case before the law that's completely incomprehensible today.

Questioning you placed me in front of a competing claim to my faith in the law. I had to return to the reasons for my vocation in order to counter your desire for another kind of justice, one that ended in defeat.

The result for me personally is that it's reinforced my convictions. For the public, I've been defeated. It's not unusual, the justice with which I identify myself suffers more defeats than the statistics for unsolved crimes reveal.

The motive behind this letter of mine sent by mail is different. You helped clarify the circumstances, at least for me. You furnished me with hints that couldn't be used as proof but useful in explaining at least how things developed in the encounter between the two of you. This was a result of questioning that often went off course and custom.

Sweetheart, his letter arrived a few days ago, written in ink on exercise paper. He said that, thinking over obsessively what we discussed in the trattoria, he'd come to understand.

It must have been some concession on my part, giving in to his efforts. I'd been prepared to tell him about episodes of my life, so he could get to know my character. I had to have come up with some detail for him. An intuition came to him one night at supper. I'll write out what he said.

> *In you there is a mix of resolution and desperation that I've met for the first time. It wasn't dust that you threw in that man's eyes on the Cengia. And I'm not asking for confirmation. I only want to let you know my conclusion. It won't have*

any effect, the case won't be opened up again, it remains sealed and archived. This evening I sprinkled some crushed hot spices on my plate. Distracted, I brushed my fingers over my eyes and jumped from my seat with the stinging. It was then that I understood.

I have to thank you for the suggestion, I couldn't have got to it by myself.

On the Cengia you sprayed that man with pepper spray from a plastic water pistol, on sale everywhere. And perhaps there wasn't any need to push him off.

The next day, the first without bars on my window, I went back to the Cengia. It's now the middle of autumn, humidity and damp have compacted the trail with less risk of falling. My footsteps crunched, the air was clear, with no clouds. The wind was picking up and filled the lungs. I wanted to go back to where I was interrupted. I don't know what I was looking for, I simply wanted to be there.

I wasn't there to return to the site of a fall and an accusation. I stopped before that.

I'd reached an escarpment and in the distance I saw a small herd of chamois. I took out my binoculars. Two males with short horns were battling for supremacy. They resolve their questions in a duel.

They were charging at each other on slopes that would have had me falling off. I stood and watched the battle. The females were waiting higher up.

The two males were perhaps brothers, having grown up together and then split up at the age they separate. You get this opposition between blood relatives in small herds.

In the silence of a still day I could hear the sounds of their breathing. It was an encounter of two bodies, their hormones reacting to the scents of the females in their brief cycle.

The two males had met at various times during the year and ignored each other. But in that precise moment, it was inevitable they would be at one another.

There's a spontaneous fidelity in the animal kingdom. Their tussle returned me to the world and the laws of nature.

Laws? Nature here had no laws; it was responding to impulse. To see a code was to misunderstand it, to see it as similar to us. Instead, I would have preferred to be like one of those two, pounding for the right to procreate, fighting to bring about birth. Their head-on collision was obeying the future's right for offspring. In that moment, and perhaps in any other, those two had put the past behind them.

Chamois don't give up after the first assaults until one surrenders at the cost of its life and not before. In the end the one more tired would find itself on lower ground and enduring the charge from above.

And that's how it was, a last head-on collision, but their horns were locked and they rolled off the slope together.

I saw them disappear, bouncing off the rocks. The muffled sound of two bodies bumping down without a cry.

I lowered the binoculars, seeing things from the right distance again.

The females had left the Cengia and it was now empty. The duel had left no sign. The page of a book containing life inside had been opened and then closed. The passion that had written it had vanished.

I went back along the narrow path between the rock

wall and the void. I was aware that my breathing was becoming heavy.

I didn't want to be one of those two chamois, I wanted to continue living.

FINIS